The Most Fragile Objects
By Alberto Chimal

Translated from Spanish by George Henson

The Most Fragile Objects
By Alberto Chimal
First Edition 2019
Original Title:

Translated from Spanish by George Henson

Original title: Los esclavos published by Editorial Almadía © 2009

Published by **Katakana editores** all rights reserved © 2019

Editor: Michele Rosen
Design: Elisa Orozco
Cover Art: *Delhi: an anatomical model advertising a pharmacy*. Colour photograph by Ben Dray, 1993. Credit: Wellcome Collection. CC BY

ISBN: 978-1-7321144-9-4

KATAKANA EDITORES CORP.
Weston FL 33331
✉ katakanaeditores@gmail.com

ALBERTO CHIMAL

Translated from the Spanish
by **George Henson**

The Most
Fragile Objects

katakana
editores

Table of Contents

Translator's Note

Cuban novelist Guillermo Cabrera Infante begins his novel *Three Trapped Tigers* with the following "warning": "The book is in Cuban. That is, written in the different dialects of Spanish that are spoken in Cuba, and writing is nothing more than an attempt to capture the human voice in flight." Similarly, it could be said that Alberto Chimal's *The Most Fragile Objects* is written in Mexican. This is not to say the entire novel is, or that a Spaniard or Colombian or any other Spanish-speaker would not understand it. They would. They would also, within a few pages, identify it as having been written by a Mexican author, not by the grammar, or even most of the vocabulary, but rather by the colloquial speech used by its characters. In this sense, much of the dialogue might be foreign to them. It is this foreignness that gives *The Most Fragile Objects*, any novel in fact, its linguistic and cultural uniqueness. Regrettably, many publishers—and more than a few translators—prefer to erase any sign of foreignness from the translation under the misguided assumption that readers are more comfortable reading texts that are more familiar than foreign.

To avert the foreign and avoid any discomfort the reader may experience, translators recur to a process known as equivalence, that is, an attempt to create "sameness" or "similarity" in the receiving language. Because many words and expressions are culturally specific to a language or dialect, however, it is difficult to reach equivalence in another language, and so the attempt to translate them results in some degree of cultural loss. For this reason, I have chosen to leave certain words and phrases in Spanish. But also, as Cabrera Infante did, in an attempt to capture the voice of the characters, at least part of it, in flight. This practice is not new. On the contrary, it is often done by translators, who place words or expressions in italics as a signal to readers that they've stumbled upon something foreign. This long-standing practice of italicizing, however, has come under scrutiny of late. Not only does Dominican-American author Junot Díaz, who writes in English, not italicize Dominican words and phrases in his texts, he advocates that other writers and translators also abandon the practice, arguing that italicizing not only signals a foreign word, but it exaggerates differences and, in doing so, has an "othering" effect. Latina author Jennifer De Leon alludes to the violence that italics inflicts, referring to them as "a barbed-wire fence."

I couldn't agree more. And so I have chosen not to use italics in my translation. (The italics that do occur in the text are the author's.) In this translation, then, you will read words and phrases that may be foreign to you. To help you along, however, and to make you a welcome participant, I've provided a glossary. Please take a moment to familiarize yourself with its words and phrases, and take them with you as you read *The Most Fragile Objects*. They are yours now. And so is this translation. Hopefully, you will experience it in a way that you otherwise would not have.

Finally, I owe a great debt to my editor Michele Rosen, whose careful eye and keen instincts made this translation better, to my publisher Omar Villasana, who believed in this project, and to Alberto Chimal, the author, for entrusting his novel to me. I am also indebted to my dear friend, Dr. Rodrigo Figueroa at New Mexico State University, not only for helping to compile the glossary but also for helping to tease out the nuances of phrases that, although familiar to me, continue to be foreign. 囝

George Henson
Monterey, California

¡ay! an exclamation equivalent to ouch! or oh! or even goodness!

barranca a ravine or gulley; while not uniquely Mexican, the barranca is important to visualizing the location of the *colonia* (shanty town) where a part of the novel takes place.

cabrón literally "a large male goat," used to refer to anything from a "cuckold husband" to "guy," "dude," "badass," "asshole," or "son-of-a-bitch." (There also exists a historical-semantic relationship between *cabrón* and Bacchus and satyrs insofar as a *cabrón* is someone who fucks people over, a fact that most Spanish-speakers are unaware of.)

chale an interjection that implies deep disappointment, used exclusively in informal situations.

chingar so important is the word *chingar*, and all its variants, to Mexican identity that Mexican poet and Nobel laureate Octavio Paz dedicated an entire chapter to it in his philosophical treatise *The Labyrinth of Solitude*, writing that its "magical power is intensified by its prohibited nature." In its infinitive form, it means "to fuck"—literally or figuratively—and the meaning of its variant forms can range from harmless to comical to violent.

la chingada "the fucked woman," or a mythical place where you send people rather than to hell, or in expressions like *me lleva la chingada* (I'll be goddamned).

hijo or hija de la chingada the "son or daughter of the fucked woman"; someone who has metaphorically no mother and therefore no morals or sense of good.

una chingadera something worthless when referring to an object or despicable when referring to an action.

chingando "fucking," as when a character says: "dale una raya pa que no esté chingando" (give him a bump so he won't be fucking [with us]).

un chingo a bunch, a whole lot, a fucking lot.

colonia literally "colony"; in Mexico a *colonia* may refer to a neighborhood or an extraofficial settlement.

comal a metal or earthenware griddle that is a mainstay in traditional Mexican kitchens, used to cook tortillas and sear meats

fonda a small, usually mom-and-pop diner, with few tables, offering homecooked meals for a very cheap price.

güey sometimes spelled "wey," from the word *buey*, meaning ox, it was originally used to refer to men who had been cockled (the implication being they had been castrated); it is roughly equivalent to "dude," but can also mean "fool." Until recently, *güey* was the domain of men and boys, but never in mixed company, at least within good families. Nowadays, women also use *güey* to refer to other women, especially among good friends.

licenciado literally "licensed" or "degreed" (equivalent to a bachelor's degree in the US); it is often used to refer to attorneys (the law degree in Mexico is an undergraduate degree) or anyone with a degree or as a courtesy title for anyone important or holding a position of authority. It can be used alone, like "señor."

no mames literally "do not suck." It is used in response to a comment or question with which you do not agree or that you find ridiculous or incredible. It can mean "get out of here," or "what the hell!"

órale pues an interjection or exclamation showing approval or agreement. Its translation is always situational. If someone says, "Nos vemos mañana" (See you tomorrow), a Mexican might say *órale pues*, meaning "Okie, dokie." In other contexts, it might mean "Hell yeah!" It may also mean "let's go!," "faster!," "move it!," or "whatever."

pedo literally "fart," but also "drunk"; used also in expressions like ¡qué pedo! (what's the big deal!).

pendejo literally a "pubic hair," but in Mexican Spanish it can mean everything from "idiot" to "jerk" to "coward" to "asshole."

perra bitch, literally and figuratively.

pinche adjective that functions as an intensifier, meaning anything from "stupid" to "God damn" to "fucking," especially before first names and also *pendejo*.

pinche ruca a disparaging way to refer to an elderly woman; adding *pinche* makes it a particularly offensive insult; may also be used to refer to any woman or to someone's girlfriend or wife.

pinche ruco masculine version of *ruca*; can be used to refer to someone's father or husband, but it's not used in this way as commonly as *ruca* is for women.

puta "whore" or "slut."

puta barata literally "cheap whore," meaning that someone is worthless or a sellout.

puta madre literally "mother whore"; equivalent of "Holy shit!"

puto literally "male whore"; used to refer to a man who is a traitor, especially to his gender and sexuality, therefore also "fag" or "coward"; also used as an adjective to mean "fucking" or "goddamn." 🈂

a)

I say my principles, and I use that word advisedly.
For they are not, like those of other women,
discovered by chance...
Choderlos de Laclos

1

Marlene switches on the lights.

2

Behind the bed are some red curtains, a little dirty and frayed on the upper edges. The Stallion's face—inexpressive, his lips always pursed and his eyelids half-closed—reddens only slightly when he gets aroused. He could be a doll, the kind with artificial hair implanted in its head and two dark glass eyes, dry and shiny. Several years ago a client told Marlene about automatons, toys with a very smooth finish, unparalleled in the design of their imitation muscles, their plastic skin, soft and fragrant, their belts and secret cogs used to control the pulses of the organ that, here and now, with *this automaton*, hasn't only become erect, suddenly and without ceremony, enormous and blind and wild, but is now inside Yuyis, who has decided to act a bit and, between groans, moves her pelvis from left to right, and back, raising and lowering it, as the bed sheets become messy and wrinkled beneath the weight of their naked bodies.

Marlene, who watches them through the eyepiece, has thought about the Stallion's stone face and the mystery that allows him to move on top of and inside Yuyis as if he were asleep or dead. But she's never formulated the question with words: when she's not thinking about the automaton, of which she only has a vague image, she thinks about an inflatable doll, its pink round mouth open and three eyelashes painted above each eye. So the only thing she can do is continue admiring, as she moves the camera in order to see everything, the Stallion's unquenchable stamina, how he attacks and attacks and attacks again, how even his speed increases rather than decreases when he and Yuyis have passed the ten-minute mark and the girl begins to complain in different way, and the automaton goes on and on, always with the same thrust, at most with a little moisture on his forehead and a hesitation, a slight hint of waning strength, on his lips, which the lens zooms in on (in an extreme close-up), as they open slightly and expose his sharpened fang, yellowed, pointed like an animal's, which despite its small size and crudeness looks much better than Yuyis' tense smile, fake, filled with square incisors that lead to red gums out of the light's reach. The girl's legs are as open as before but she's extremely tired: having surrendered to a force different than the Stallion's, eager to finish.

3

"This is where I do my stuff," Marlene says.

Surprised, the two distributors—who came here especially from the capital—examine the quality of the sets stored in one of the rooms upstairs. They've already seen the assortment of movies: a catalog of more than two hundred titles manufactured here, without interference from anyone.

"We do everything here," Yuyis says, but her nudity disturbs the two men, so Marlene tells her to shut up. The men don't relax: besides, Yuyis is chained by the throat to a metal ring crudely attached to the concrete floor. There are similar rings in different rooms throughout the house.

Marlene unchains her.

16

"Get out," she orders, and Yuyis leaves, walking slightly hunched over, her eyes fixed on the floor. The two men have already seen her in many of her best scenes.

4

The man's a pizza delivery guy, the blurb on the box would say if the boxes had writing, or photos, or anything else. His sudden appearance at the house, on the edge of a highway, that divides two dusty streets, is a little odd, even more so because the house is lit up with red, blue, green and yellow lights, like the window of a five and dime, and because the phone numbers painted on the gas tank of his motorcycle and on the pizza box, as if to attract orders, are from another city and have more digits. When the man rings the doorbell, Yuyis opens the door and immediately slides her tongue between her lips, after which the man (who, although a pizza delivery guy, is shirtless, his firm torso glistening with oil) throws the pizza box to the floor, rips off Yuyis' blouse and throws her on a bed that's right behind them and is the only piece of furniture in the house.

5

Marlene no longer looks the same as when she made movies, but she's still attractive. So, when she's alone, to remind herself that she's still desirable, she allows herself a single coquetry: when she sits at her worktable, in the middle of the house's empty dining room, she moves from side to side in the chair, allowing the hem of her skirt to move up her thighs. In another time, this studied clumsiness allowed her to please more than one man; now it allows her to remember and sometimes laugh at Yuyis, who doesn't understand the play of insinuation and discovery that takes place right before her eyes when she observes her.

Marlene sits at the table, most frequently, to do the books. Before, she would dedicate a certain amount of time to writing scripts, but now she only writes when she wants to film one of her "personal" projects, which always involve elaborate acting from Yuyis and a few actors from her most select "stable." People nowadays don't want fucking with storylines, just sex, and not even with well-directed framing or professional lighting: nowadays videos have to look like they're done by fans, quick, furtive glances, like those Yuyis steals of Marlene when she sees her sit down.

6

"I'll be right back," Marlene says.

"Okay."

"Perra," she adds, before closing the door from the outside.

Yuyis, whose skin is flabby and lean at the same time, with opaque eyes and long, bony fingers—she always hides her hands—spends lots of days alone, with nothing to do, while Marlene runs errands. She doesn't care if she's left tied up or loose: she likes evenings the least, which, in addition to being lonely and barely warm enough, are filled with smelly dust that's always floating in the air. Even worse, they're boring: cars don't even go by the house. When there are, Yuyis likes to listen to them: she's able to anticipate their arrival as the sound of the motor grows louder, and it never ceases to amaze her that when they finally drive by, when the sound is the loudest, they've already gone. From the hum of their engines, she's figured out that their departure sounds an inverse progression toward nothing. It's almost, Yuyis thinks, what being inside a car must be like.

Suddenly, while Yuyis amuses herself lying on her back on the floor, listening to the nonstop hum ringing in her head, while rubbing her eyes, a car approaches: almost inaudible, slow, it's there, in her ears, for several seconds, before she decides—she's not chained—to move.

Almost immediately, as soon as she decides, she leaps out of bed, runs to the window, but remembers that her lips aren't painted, so she drops to the floor to look for a lipstick.

When she finally finds it, and puts it on, and takes off her bra, and puts on her heels, and opens the window, the car has already gone by and is getting farther away.

For a long time, in a shrill voice (her idiot's voice, Marlene says), Yuyis screams insults into the air.

7

"Your, uh…, spell…, what was it, yeah, spell?" Yuyis says, and she shuts up. She looks to one side then to the other. The pointed hat falls off the actor's head.

"'Your spell turns even the best woman bad,' idiot," Marlene says, furious. Yuyis doesn't get up. "Never mind, don't say anything, forget it."

Standing, the actor looks between his legs.

"And you," Marlene barks," go get the Stillson wrench."

"Gimme a second, and I will," the actor grumbles, but obeys.

8

So, now locked in the house's bathroom (which is acting as a hotel bathroom), without the possibility of escape, Yuyis discovers that the two policewomen restraining her, each clutching one of her arms, are in reality sex slaves that belong to the captain, who have lost their beauty after years of nonstop sex and ardent torture, which has rendered them fat and flabby. And so the man is now looking for a new victim. Yuyis (although her name here is Trixy, or Trixxxy) begs for help, but the two women will obey their master to the death, even if it means that they'll both be discarded like trash to make way for a new favorite. Now they force her kneel down beside them. Now they rip off her clothes. Now they tell her the words that she must say when she opens the bathroom door. Will Yuyis be able to escape her destiny, or will she find pleasure in surrendering to the animal desires of Captain Sex.

9

Yuyis herself has asked Marlene for most of her outfits. Depending on her mood, she might want anything from the scantiest to the most modest to the most outrageous. And Marlene, who has "abused" Yuyis, not only more than anyone else, but "much more than imaginable," almost always allows herself to succumb to a feeling akin to guilt, made up of equal parts of relief and being fed up: after all, she's the one who educated her, who trained her in submission and has kept her imprisoned from the beginning.

So she's a little reluctant, and sometimes she backs up what she says with threats or beatings, but eventually she gives in to the begging and crying and gives her presents in big boxes, wrapped in newspaper to give the false impression that they contain some cheap trinket. Yuyis pretends not to know what's inside as she rips off the paper; instead, making their way to the closet are a white tutu, whose ruffles fold upward and close like a lazy Susan in order to expose everything below the waist; red and yellow feathers to wear on her head, attached to the back, or as decoration to very ornate G-strings; an electric-blue cowgirl suit, consisting of a hat, belt, holsters and boots; a bear costume that splits suddenly into two halves, front and back, that fall on the floor; a hoopskirt and kimono open in the front; several pairs of denim pants, with and without holes, with and without studs; tailored suits in stark colors that—according to Marlene—appeal to certain viewers; twenty t-shirts, each one a different color, with the words *PUTA BARATA* written in sequins; four rubber outfits: black, red, white and blue (each one complete with masks with mouths painted on and two holes for breathing) that stick to your skin, are extremely hot and hard to wash.

Yuyis stares at them in the closet. Both she and Marlene dream about putting them on and taking them off in front of the camera. But Marlene dreams about them with much more tenacity and resolve: In most cases, Yuyis is already asking for more clothes before she's debuted her most recent acquisitions, and in this a central trait of her character can be seen: an inclination toward boredom, which Marlene must combat during almost every take once the first few minutes of filming have passed.

10

The two men, one of whom is in front, and the other in back, introduced themselves as rich and famous producers.

"You have everything it takes to be a star."
"Really big."
"Don't you want to be?
"No, I mean yes," Yuyis said. "Yes, I do."
"A new car every year," said the one whose pants were now off, "and a house in Acapulco..."
"Ay, sí, papito."
"And all the men you want?"
"And what do I have to do?" Yuyis asked, as the second man took his clothes off.

(The movie's title was *El Macho Mágico* and was to be the first in a series about a very daring character who would enter the most unusual houses and buildings, alone, or with friends that he brought along, and stage orgies and have sex with the woman of his choosing, because his powers of attraction and seduction were larger than the size of his member: each time his member was shown it was surrounded by strobe lights, and the victims would look as if they were having an orgasm just from looking at it.)

11

Of course, it's important not to forget Yuyis' coworkers, her girl-friends, sisters, all of whom who have it better than her: in addition to more agreeable working conditions, none of them lives in the house. Yuyis suspects that they don't even live in town and that they come to their shoots by bus or by other means from far away.

Yuyis doesn't see them often, restricted as she is to her room and the few other places she's allowed to go when she's not filming, and to mention them all would require making a list of a certain length: from Abelina—"the fat midget who's dumb and full of herself," as Yuyis calls her—who doesn't appear in a lot of productions because of her size but is given star billing because she co-starred in *Distant Tampons*, to Zorayda, a cleaning woman at the local clinic whose name is really Fabiola who cleans up and helps with the props, and whom it took Marlene more than a year to convince to step in front of the camera for her first takes. In any case, Yuyis doesn't keep track of all the people she knows or those with whom she exchanges glances and shares Marlene's orders. Some might be interesting people—there's the transsexual Frida, for example, who has so many implants that touching her anywhere on her body produces the most curious and disturbing sensations—but deep down Yuyis feels the same contempt for all of them: when she's talking to them, when she has to kiss them or be kissed by them or bury her face between their legs, when there's a break between takes and they get together in the corner to eat nude while the camera is moved and the lights changed, when they're paid and she sees them get dressed and leave through one of the doors that are invariably off-limits to her; all of them remind her that her position is special: that, despite all the gifts and caresses Marlene provides, she's still a prisoner.

"Your situation is really weird," a certain Pepina told her once. Pepina is a girl with small, saggy breasts, a ring in her nose, and two misshapen Chinese characters tattooed in black and red on her stomach covered in stretch marks; Yuyis never knew her name, but she remembers her anyway because the two of them did a scene in which they played with vegetables. "What's the deal, does she pay you, do you do what she says because she gives you dough, or does it turn you on?"

They had to repeat the scene several times because (although to this day Yuyis still doesn't know why) Pepina's innocent, yet extremely stupid, lines infuriated Yuyis, and every once in a while, instead of moving the carrot or the celery stalk or whatever she was supposed to move, she would mumble:

"You're the weird one, *hija de la chingada*," after which Marlene would yell cut, sigh, get annoyed, scream at her, pull the cucumber or the banana out, wave it at her, then hit her in the face or chest with it.

12

"Wash yourself good," Marlene has always told her, and she's happy to obey, especially when she's allowed to use the old fiberglass tub: she likes watching the foam, how the water changes colors, the occasional residue, tiny, fleeting, infinitely flexible, that rises to the surface or gathers on the bottom of the tub.

During one of her rare trips out of town, Marlene stumbled upon a kiosk in a metro station that sold pirated copies of her movies. The DVDs were in plastic bags. She didn't recognize the distributor's logo because of the really bad printing job, but she did recognize Yuyis, pictured with her legs opened, two fingers on her lips, her body completely shaved.

"Ma'am."

She'd taken the photo herself: perhaps on the back there was one of the fat chick, the old woman, and the transsexual who rounded off the cast.

"Lady."

The kid who was selling the movies was about to throw her out when Marlene remembered that a respectable woman doesn't stop in front of a porn kiosk, and she left, laughing under her breath as if she'd done something mischievous.

Marlene shares a problem with Yuyis: she can't concentrate in front of the TV or go two minutes without changing the channel, looking away or obsessing about details she didn't catch in whatever she was watching. Seated at her feet, Yuyis fidgets, just as edgy, but Marlene doesn't pay attention and instead gets up, turns on the radio or the stereo, or opens the door to the room, leaves and closes the door.

Then, alone, she goes upstairs to one of the rooms on the second floor, which is completely off limits to Yuyis. Marlene likes to think that it's in part an act of mercy: Yuyis is barefoot—and naked—almost all the time, and the floor is concrete, and just like the walls, is full of irregularities and rough spots. (In reality, the only finish-out after the actual construction are pieces of plastic or wood where the windows were going to be and the light cables that run from the kitchen to the outside wall off the house.)

Now in the room, Marlene follows the cord until she finds the light (she usually leaves it on the floor next to the hole where the door frame was supposed to be), picks it up, turns it on and, holding it up high as if it were a candle, and lingers to admire the shelves where she keeps her collection of original video.

They're all there, from the first to the last, in chronological order, labeled with convenient titles that she takes time to invent but that don't always appear on the boxes they are going to be sold in. She knows that it's useless to save a "master," as one of her buyers says, because they'll make the copies they want and sell them at the price they want, where and when they want. But each title, written in permanent marker on the corresponding cardboard or plastic box, brings back memories: sounds, smells, movements, skin colors and marks, and especially the many voice commands, which she can no longer associate with specific moments but have always been in all of her work, in all of the long sessions: telling the actresses to open their legs, the actors to close their mouth, to lie down, stand up, concentrate, say the few lines they have: Marlene remembers a reprimand here, a scolding there, and smiles as she stares longer and longer at *The Master's Bitch, Courtesans of Pleasure 2, The Eye of the Monkey*, or any of the hundreds of titles.

Marlene always ends these visits by pointing the light at the still-vacant shelves, which allow her to think long into the future.

15

The plot of No Balls *revolves around Adrián López, who could be a stallion but suffers from childhood trauma, because of which he's afraid of everything and needs to learn to show his stuff to women. He's an inexpressive actor, and his panicked look is the same as all his other looks, but regardless his problem is forgotten a few minutes after the action begins, when he sees Yuyis and, without moving a single muscle in his face, rapes her repeatedly, in several positions and for different pretexts, during the next sixty or seventy minutes.*

16

"What do we need?" Marlene asks, pencil and notebook in hand.

"Eggs."

"What else?"

"Milk and cream."

"Are we out?"

"Strawberry jam, ham, cheese, toilet paper."

"Did you already use it all?"

"Well I have to shit."

"Shut up, don't be…"

"You shut up."

"¡Me lleva la chingada…!" Marlene shouts and jumps on Yuyis. "Didn't I just tell you to shut up? Didn't I tell you to shut up?"

The girl can scarcely protect herself with her arms.

"Perra," Marlene says, hitting her with a closed fist, trying to hit her on the head. "Pinche ruca. Puta barata."

Marlene stops and pushes her away with so much force that Yuyis falls on the floor.

Yuyis grows pale but responds:

"No."

"No? I'll show you no," Marlene says, and picks her up from the floor, puts her on her feet, and begins to push her toward the living room door. Yuyis screams, wiggles, works her way free, tries to leave the kitchen through the other door to escape to her room, but Marlene grabs her by the hair, causing her to scream as she drags her back and stops her. Yuyis turns around and kicks her in the stomach. Marlene responds with a kick between the legs and, after causing her to fall a third time, pins her to the floor under her weight and pushes her face against the dirty, cracked tiles. Every time Yuyis manages to get free, Marlene slams her to the floor. The girl finally gives up and begins to cry.

"Now you're gonna go to the store and buy everything we need."

"I don't know where it is."

"You can't get lost; you go down the street to where it says 'Groceries.' You do know how to read, don't you?"

"No."

"I know you know how."

"I don't want to go."

"You're going. I'll give you money and you'll buy everything."

"No," Yuyis says again, still sobbing.

"And if you don't get it, don't come back."

"But I'll have to go outside."

"Of course, you moron, that's the point, that you go outside."

"But I can't!"

Marlene laughs.

"And why not?" she says, while banging her against the floor again. "Because you're naked?" Another blow. "Is that why?"—she hits her again. "If you want, I'll dress you."

Yuyis lets out a very long and prolonged howl that, when over, turns into convulsive crying. Her tears fall and mix with the dust.

After a moment, Marlene relaxes and finally allows herself to stand and look up. Yuyis' skin doesn't seem to have been hurt, which is important because in a few hours several actors and actresses will arrive, and she'll have to add continuity to several scenes from the day before. It's not that Marlene cares that a lot about the quality of her product, but she considers it unnecessary to go beyond certain limits of shoddiness and apathy.

Yuyis stops crying and falls asleep on the floor. Marlene wonders if she should cover her, but then decides that the night is warm enough, and it wouldn't be good to show too much affection after a scene like that. She steps over her without stepping on her, picks up the pencil and notebook, jots down the shopping list, tears out the page, grabs her purse, and leaves. Before walking to the store, she locks the door from the outside.

17

One time, the phone rang and Yuyis (who is strictly forbidden to do so) took a gamble and answered it.

"Hello?" a voice said.

Nervous, Yuyis laughed. Then she let out a meaningless sound.

"Hello?"

Yuyis felt the vibration of the receiver next to her ear and had an idea.

"Hello?"

After one or two attempts, however, she decided that the idea was impractical and that the shape of the receiver was too uncomfortable even for the sole task of holding it with her thighs or between her breasts.

18

On another of her trips, Marlene had the opportunity to attend to a party in honor of several filmmakers. They were in a border city, in the huge if rather rustic home belonging to a distributor, and while a director was barbecuing, the others chatted around a stone fountain. As on other occasions, Marlene noticed that more than a few of them were looking at her strangely or with outright rejection. But all she had to do was introduce herself as the creator of certain very successful films—the three installments of *Chicas Gone Wild*, for example, or *Face Cream*—to receive, if not acclaim, at least a gesture of approval or surprise.

Only one of them insulted her out loud:

"Lesbian." But deep-down Marlene hadn't gone in search of anyone's approval, and she ended up on the fringes of their conversations, holding a bottle of beer and a plate of meat.

19

A priest and two nuns have gone to the house of a dying elderly man to give him holy unction. But the priest confuses the bottle of oil with one that contains a potion made by a witch, and when he applies it to the forehead of the old man, the latter not only comes to, but exhibits a stallion-like erection and the manners of a Billy goat that frighten everyone. While crossing himself, the priest applies the same concoction and, beneath his cassock, as if activated by a spring, his own member stands at attention, demanding action. The two nuns grow even more terrified:

"¡Ay, cabrón!" says Yuyis, who's playing one of the nuns.

Quick applications of the preparation turn the two—predictably—into burning and insatiable females. Soon, the four come together in every conceivable position and call the rest of the nuns and priests back at their convent. They all arrive at the house next to the highway in the back of a stake-bed truck, which seems a little odd, not unlike the rather large number of priests in relation to the nuns; it also seems odd that a character—Marlene—who doesn't reappear, opens the door for them. As soon as they enter the room, they immediately receive the anointing that prepares them not for death but for a long night of pleasure, after which nothing else matters and the action in some way stops: there are no more plot twists, and almost all of the remaining shots are close-ups, one after the other, without explanation, of blowjobs given by Yuyis.

(Horny Nuns is the title of this movie.)

Marlene returns with the groceries and other things she's bought. She opens the door to go in and closes it behind her. She's tired. Soon, when Yuyis has deposited the house's garbage in the container, she'll have to take it out and carry it to the dumpster, which is a block away from City Hall. And then she'll have to return to some unfinished tasks, which won't leave her time for anything else. She'll have to make one of many inconsequential but unavoidable decisions, which she didn't foresee when she began this stage of her life. When she's tired, all it takes is a single order for Yuyis to start preparing dinner: the girl has no talent for cooking but knows how to follow orders and is able to passably prepare most of the recipes that Marlene has taught her. However, given that she's not allowed to even wear an apron, all the meals she's allowed to prepare are cold, which creates a deep and inexplicable sense of anxiety in Marlene. Without a doubt (she read in a magazine) it's due to some trauma from her childhood; but she doesn't like to think about such things and, in any case, the memory of the only time that Yuyis—she's truly a poor dumb thing—tried to cook a pair of eggs sunny-side up is much fresher: a few drops of boiling grease popped onto one of her shoulders and left a small but very visible scar. Perhaps she should have considered an exception to her very strict rule about nudity. What would have happened, Marlene always wonders, if the grease had hit her breasts, her face, her sex?

She turns on the television, which emits a hollow and distant voice and a series of indecipherable images. Without energy even to grab the remote, Marlene calls out to Yuyis. "Cereal with milk," she says.

"One of these days she's gonna to be a star. Because of this, I mean. You can tell she has, how can I say it, presence…"

Marlene doesn't understand.

"Presence?"

"She has it. You understand? She does it with one or however many, in front, from behind, in every position…"

"That's garbage," Marlene replies, as she presses the stop button on the camera and yanks the tape out. "Pure garbage. Pure bull-shit. Caca. Garbage."

But then she puts it back in the camera, finishes the scene, and shortly thereafter she's negotiating payment with the man, who gives her a wad of bills as an advance.

22

At seven in the morning, when she gets up and starts to get ready, Marlene quickly enters Yuyis' room, unchains her if she's bound, turns on the stereo that's on the bureau, and plays an exercise CD. There's never any other disk in the player, and in fact Yuyis is for-bidden to even touch the device, so the same pulsating, monoto-nous dance music always comes on at a volume that makes the windows shake. "Boom-boom music," Marlene calls it, but she has no idea who plays the songs or how old they are: she bought the disc at the only counterfeit stand in town, several years ago, when she realized that Yuyis needed to exercise.

And she pushes the bedspread to the side, jumps out of bed and begins. This way she won't get fat, Marlene says to herself ev-ery morning, while she watches her jump in place (such that her breasts swing and bounce against her body) before moving on to pushups, stretching, abs, and a little running in place, as in an aer-obic dance routine. She often records takes with the camera.

When Yuyis finishes, she reports immediately to the kitchen to fix breakfast, and then Marlene thinks of another unpleasant side of the girl's nudity: she reeks of sweat. But the problem is due, once again, to her own lack of planning: she's unwilling to get up earlier to give Yuyis time to bathe. And, on the other hand, even though the stereo can be programmed to turn on automatically at seven in the morning, Marlene not only lacks the patience required to learn how, she wants to be there. For a long time, she enjoyed the frightened and disconcerted look on Yuyis' face as the music woke her up (and occasionally the task of forcing her to wake up), but some time ago Yuyis stopped being startled when she stirs. Perhaps she's grown accustomed to waking up alone a little before seven; or so Marlene hopes, making sure, whenever possible, that Yuyis goes to bed after doing the hardest chores: perhaps one day she'll not be able to wake up.

23

Prince Charming, first, gives the impression that he'll pay attention to Yuyis the fairy, who not only hasn't shed her dress and muslin wings, but has turned her attention to fellating him with enthusiasm and patience. But when she finishes and stands up to kiss him on the mouth, he moves away and tells her that he's actually gay, then proves it with a long kiss and a quick fuck with his squire. Disappointed, Yuyis joins the two in a second romp and then receives a welcome visit from another fairy, who until that moment hadn't been seen but is already naked and aroused. All this happens in the same bedroom, decorated with cardboard trees, with all the furniture hidden beneath white cloth.

A man comes to the house to visit Marlene and Yuyis is ordered to hide. And she does. As they're talking they walk toward the door of the room where Yuyis, squatting down on the floor, can hear this part of their conversation:

"Seriously, señora, you're still doing your little thing?"

"I don't know what you're talking about."

"You're still doing the same thing."

"I don't understand, licenciado."

"Don't pretend."

"Look, if you want anything…"

"Like what?"

"I'm already paying Sr. Gervasio."

"Now you're going to have to pay me too. I'm in the Deputy Director's office now."

"So, why…?"

(A pause.)

"Because I deserve it."

"No, licenciado, why should I have to pay you?"

"Because if you don't, your little theater here will cease to exist. The police will come, they'll take you away, give you thirty or forty years, we'll seize the house, and whatever else I can think of. You know I don't like you. And I don't like blowjobs."

(Another pause.)

"Wouldn't you like to fuck, licenciado?

(Another pause.)

"Not me, licenciado"

Another pause, and suddenly the room door opens.

Yuyis barely has time to get out of the way and let Marlene and a short bald man with a gray mustache and thick glasses pass. He was wearing a bolo tie and boots under his polyester pants.

"This is Yuyis. Look at her. She's healthy and …

"Is she one of your…?

"...actresses."

"Why is she naked?"

"She's also a whore."

Although Yuyis used it often, she didn't know the meaning of the word "whore." But still she would have said "You're the whore" or something similar if Marlene hadn't yanked her up. She ordered her to touch her feet with her hands, stand in front of the deputy director with her hands on her hips and then behind her head. Yuyis had done it all before and obeyed as always.

"Are you her manager?"

Another pause.

"No, said Marlene, she's just staying here, that's all."

""Don't lie to me, Madam."

Yuyis could have said that she'd always been there, but she didn't say anything.

"I'm not lying, licenciado. She, Yuyis, owes me a favor, isn't that right?"

Yuyis understood that she should say:

"Yes."

"You're going to pay me by doing a favor for the licenciado."

"What?"

"Go on, quick, on your knees."

"How old is she?"

Another pause. Marlene didn't answer, but Yuyis, while getting down on her knees, saw her make an expression that she had never seen her make. She was smiling, but only on one side of her face; and her eyebrow on the opposite side was so arched that (Yuyis thought) that it left her eye abandoned, as if floating in an empty space of skin and makeup.

"Oh, okay. Are you sure?"

"A gesture of good will, licenciado."

"There," he said, pointing to Yuyis' bed.

"Get in bed," Marlene ordered.

Yuyis gets up again and walks, unsure, in front of them. She lays on the animal bedspread and wonders if there was something she didn't fully understand because she'd never been filmed in her own room before. And, besides, the camera wasn't there, not to mention the man didn't look like an actor: not only was he not tall enough, but when he took off his shirt he exposed a torso that was both thin and flabby: with visible ribs and ugly folds of flesh beneath them.

"I'll look the other way this time," the deputy director said later, as he pulled on his trousers. "But start putting the money aside, you hear me? To be honest, it's... How can I say it? Not very good, okay? Not very good."

25

There are several lies in what's been told to this point: the most important is that Marlene's career in pornographic movies is much less important and prosperous than has been indicated—in fact, it ended a long time ago—, and although she does film, very occasionally, tapes in which Yuyis appears, almost all of the projects she's undertaken (and that cost her money she's never been able to recoup) have stayed, unedited, on the first floor of her house, actually half-built, hidden in the drawers of a file cabinet. Stored in the same room are the boxes of films that she does distribute.

Marlene goes upstairs, opens the file cabinet, picks out a tape and goes downstairs to watch it. When it's over, she goes and puts it back in its place, and while doing so she thinks about the actors she hires (actually very rarely), and who think she's crazy, or about the four curtains that she used in her first films. These are still on the floor of a room adjacent to the one with the boxes, and no one has touched them in years. They rotted a long time ago.

The following should also be mentioned: sometimes, while she's walking downstairs, Marlene stops midway on the stairs;

goes up again; goes to a plastic cooler she keeps hidden in a third room, which is always empty except for a vial in which she keeps her cocaine: what little she's able to get and which she must invariably ration for several months.

She takes the vial downstairs to Yuyis' room, who's usually already asleep. She wakes her up, sits down next to her, and begins to undress her.

"Madre," complains the girl, who's just turned sixteen, and in fact wouldn't normally have a reason to resent being awakened so abruptly.

But she knows she shouldn't resist when Marlene, who's put a little white powder on her gums and her vaginal labia, does her thing with her. And she knows that she should already be uncovered, and prepared, when Marlene takes the two-headed dildo out from the drawer in the bureau that holds the stereo.

If Yuyis hasn't gotten behind, she has permission to continue to complain: she can say "Hey, I'm sleepy," or that she doesn't feel like it, or that a person doesn't do that—whatever she wants to give the impression that she's resisting—until Marlene inserts the toy in her and inserts the other end in herself, to begin the back-and-forth. But then she must stay silent. She can't say anything while Marlene penetrates her and penetrates herself, with increasing force, among moans and words here and there.

"Pinche madre," she says today when she feels the head of the dildo. She doesn't say more.

Yuyis must remain silent even when Marlene starts to scream, groan with rage, and hurt her. She usually prefers to close her eyes and think about something to distract her—like music she likes, that she hears from time to time on TV, or about the dresses she has in her closet, which are much less numerous and expensive than previously stated—but on other occasions she keeps them very open and watches Marlene's face, so similar to hers, or the ceiling beyond her face, the pieces of paint that are starting to fall, the dust that's collected on the light cord. 🈙

We obey, without considering
what will one day come
of all this thoughtless obedience.

Robert Walser

26

Latour opens the door.

27

Mundo screams and curses, but makes no effort to enter. Because he's out in the mud and the rain, he'd get the floor dirty, and besides he smells bad. And he's incapable of disobeying a direct order:

"Stay there," Latour told him, and Mundo is conditioned from years of relentlessly evil training, refined torture, and spiritual exercises; he has turned into, as was the plan from the beginning, a submissive and almost unconscious creature. So he doesn't enter: lying on his back, he turns from one side to the other. He screams for forgiveness, curses his status as an unworthy and wretched creature. He then raises his legs as high as he can and lets his feet fall into the puddle. The dirty water explodes, rising in the direction opposite to the movement of rain, and breaks into numerous drops that trace tiny arcs before ending up on the ground, or on Mundo's stretched-out body, or in his open mouth or in his eyes, which don't blink.

Several minutes pass. It continues to rain. In the distance, a car drives by, or a child plays in his own puddles, or someone, it's unknown if it's a male or female, can be barely seen, approaching along a street parallel to the home. Mundo struggles to keep Latour's interest, whom is hard to please and doesn't like to repeat acts of humiliation. The sun traces its slow, invisible arc, over the storm clouds; while Mundo prays, he pounds his stomach, stirs his feces into the mud, rolls over (of course), insults people he loved at one time: these are customary tantrums, prescribed even, but they serve to combat boredom.

During all this time Latour watches him. When it's about to get dark, he goes back inside the house, stays there a moment, goes out again and gives a new order. Mundo rises, walks towards his master with his eyes fixed on the ground and kneels when he reaches him.

28

"When he came here, you may find it hard to believe, but he was quite independent and very wild, very proud."

The old man, who is the host of the party, looks at Mundo, who's been lying on the floor with his eyes closed. A waiter carrying a tray approaches the three men and stops. Latour motions him to move on and the waiter obeys, trying not to step on Mundo.

"Very wild, you say?" asks the old man, and Latour realizes that his curiousness is in fact envy: even there, in that secure environment, few dare to go so far.

29

Mundo is " Latour's ugly brother, his pathetic, detestable double": his property. As a rule, he lives naked and curled up in a ball, next to the kitchen door; it is no exaggeration to say that he is an animal. In addition to the usual treatment, he's received (every Friday,

Sunday, and Tuesday since coming into Latour's life) additional torture, meted out by the cruelest of masters. One can't but feel pity seeing him raise his head—dirty and covered with matted hair, almost always full of every imaginable filth—when he hears his master's footsteps. It's even more heartbreaking to see him run on all fours, rub against Latour's legs, beg for his attention, or at least try, with rasping, inarticulate moans.

"Idiot!" Latour yells, and Mundo answers back:

"Idiot," without abandoning his position or caresses, then going on with a hundred more words, in a dozen languages, which Latour taught him and that describe him. Most are from languages he doesn't even know—kundel, which means "mongrel" in Polish, kichigai, or "imbecile" in Japanese, and achterlijke, Dutch for "retarded"—but every word is heard in a clear and resounding way, as if they were made of glass or metal.

30

"What a horrible thing," says the actress. Nervous, she lifts her glass to take a sip and almost spills it.

"There are better ones."

"Better?"

"Of course. One should never overestimate beings like this. Look what a beast. He's carrion."

"What are you talking about? Aren't you supposed to be...? What is he doing?"

Latour enjoys the woman's confusion so much that he doesn't answer immediately. Instead he deigns, for the first time in the whole conversation, to look down, to see what Mundo is doing.

"Don't pay him any attention. He loves being mistreated. He takes pride in it. Allow me." And Mundo doesn't quite manage to lick the shoe that kicks him in the mouth.

31

Occasionally, Mundo is content to do nothing, to let time pass. Then he plays at suspending his thoughts and just being an animal. He doesn't try to name the objects that surround him in the house or recognize anyone who isn't Latour: this way everyone looks the same, imprecise faces, weak, incomprehensible voices. Someone walks up and pricks him with something. Mundo falls asleep. Later he wakes up and is somewhere else, but he attempts to forget his awareness of the fact and merely surrender, like an animal, like before the stranger came to stick him.

32

Latour writes, in pencil, on cream-colored paper: *Yes, Latour is perverse; perversity is a virtue. On the scale of things, skill and sincerity are rarely equal to those things that his soul's nature recognizes.*

Latour hits hard and knows how to hit in places that hurt. Latour knows how to subjugate and order.

Latour believes that everyone would like to give orders, and those who deny it are merely afraid, aware of the nothingness of every being and every effort at living, or possess an even greater desire to obey, to disappear into someone else's will.

The beings that are his property are always awaiting, in need of his orders, his fury, and his rare queries. But Latour doesn't need them. More than once he's killed them, has disposed of their bodies and continued with his own life.

With Latour, every story is true, as are all the tales of pain, torture, restraints, accessories, appliances.

Latour isn't the terrible god his slaves worship; rather something higher: different.

And Latour is simple: he knows that all his games are useless, a new ugliness in that design that has always been horrible and is, as always, devoid of meaning.

He then tears up the sheet, burns it, urinates on it, or feeds it to Mundo. Never underestimate the importance of arbitrary gestures.

33

"E," Mundo says. "E,e,e,e,e"

He's on the floor of a library, in another house, dressed only in a mask that resembles the head of a mouse. Persuaded, he tries to eat a piece of cheese that Latour has placed next to him on the rug. The mask doesn't have any openings.

34

Due to the drugs he's been given, the hypnotic suggestion or some other procedure, Mundo doesn't remember much about his life before meeting Latour. He's grown accustomed to not thinking about that and, in fact, to not think about almost anything else: when he's not sleeping, eating, defecating, or engaged in some immediate task, he repeats to himself, in silence, a few words, over and over, to prevent his mind from wandering or becoming distracted. At first, he used slogans: "I obey Latour," "Latour is my owner," and other similar ones, but for some time he has simply formed lists of individual words: "dog, cat, cow, helicopter, telephone," "sixteen, rose water, concrete, saber," which he goes over during the long hours when Latour ignores him. He may be on the patio, which is little more than the cement plates that cover the ground, a pile of rusty objects in the background, and the puddles left by the rain; he may wander the hallways inside, which lead only to rooms that look alike to Mundo, full of objects he's forbidden to touch. It is always better to stay crouched on the cement, lying face down on the tiles, standing inside the empty closet under the stairs, his eyes fixed on some point, going over his words. Sometimes he whispers them; at other times he spells them out in silence, with a persistence that he isn't aware of, but that Latour himself would consider admirable.

35

"Asking him to clean," Latour explains, "is boring. He's constant-ly doing it with his tongue and never stops. It doesn't matter if it's a floor or a toilet."

"Not very original," the minister says.

"I must confess that it's not his only fault," and he suddenly feels anger at these little men. "Hey, piece of shit," He says to Mundo, "do you know how disgusting you are, how many faults you have?"

36

Latour isn't isolated. Even if he's traveling from one house to an-other, even if he's at one of the most remote cabins, he's accus-tomed to using phones, computers, or any device necessary to take care of his affairs. None of which matters to him; he gives only the minimum orders to keep things running smoothly. People who are more devoted than he take care of what's necessary, in reality; and in the satisfaction that this power gives him, both omnipotent and irresponsible, Latour discovered, a long time ago, the first sign that allowed him to exposed his true interests.

Other signs came later: the tedium of life among those who were supposedly his equals, the number and unbearable stubbornness of his inferiors, the countless restrictions that hinder the most creative ways to exercise power, the shame imposed, and in many cases sought and cultivated, by those who purported to share his hobbies.

Latour's "virtual" life—in the most vulgar sense of word—is as follows: when he is bored and comes to desire something other than his daily routines, Latour goes online and searches for places where fetishists, pornographers, and others like him, get together to brag, tell stories, or congregate. Latour has read a lot of what is written in these spaces: simple stories of hookups and played-out fantasies; he has come to know their ordinariness, their timidity, and their lack of imagination; when he grows bored of reading, he hides behind one of his many assumed names, writes accounts of his own life and his time with Mundo and others, accounts of their acts and games, and he sends them to his electronic readers. They are never successful, because—according to a boastful and paternalistic correspondent—they come off as "unexciting." This has made Latour think that none of the people he chats with on the computer has a toy as good as Mundo, and that, more likely than not, they are all just armchair fantasizers, pitiful beings who'll never act according to their wishes and who live with enormous guilt, convinced of their own evilness, fantasizing about what they've never even tried to understand.

37

"Mundo," Mundo says through the receiver, and on the other end of the line someone grows impatient. "Mundo, Mundo, Mundo."

Latour frowns slightly and hangs up the phone. It's almost three in the morning.

38

In the city where the house is, there is also a very exclusive park, guarded by armed guards. There, Latour can take Mundo, on a leash and wearing a muzzle, and show him to other pet owners.

"He has the perfect degree of... how do you say in Spanish?"

"Neglect? Excuse me, your daughter... is she your daughter?"

Mundo sniffs the little girl and pretends to wag his tail. If Latour were interested in the matter, he would say that his slave likes this role especially, this part of his duties: he's good at imitating the innocence of animals (the *irrationality* of animals, the *irresponsibility* of animals).

The little girl allows him to do it and then gives an order to her own pet, naked and equipped just like Mundo but much older. The pet lifts its leg, much higher than seems possible considering the appearance of its body, and urinates on Mundo.

39

When his master orders, Mundo can bathe himself, dress normally, comb his hair, put on shoes and a tie. He can also use all the bathrooms in the house. Only the ones in very tight spaces upset him, which are precisely those that Latour prefers to assign to him.

"No, that's what you're here for, so I can tell you when and where," and he doesn't allow him go anywhere else to relieve himself (it's the term he uses), nor does he allow him to return to his animalesque positions or stain his clothes. "No, I told you. That's your bathroom and you have to use your bathroom," and so on, sometimes, for hours, as Mundo grows more and more agitated, and wiggles and bends over, and ends up soiling himself anyway, or by crawling on the ground in search of forgiveness.

Latour has also recorded the history of Mundo in writing. Not as a sign of appreciation or deference: on the contrary, he's also left a record (at least for a time) of the others, those who preceded Mundo since Latour earned the right to make decisions about his own life and the attention he would pay to his interests.

In addition to the sordid, sad, but also predictably detailed report about the recruitment of Mundo (the cars at night, the masked assassins, the cries of panic from the trunk, the different screams that marked his entrance into the house), Latour has a fondness for evoking those who guided him: his teachers in the arts of subduing or breaking someone's will, as well as of inflicting largely unbearable pleasures. (The latter, even more than conventional torture, are the real tools of submission.)

His teachers were numerous, and while not all collaborated personally in Mundo's education, nor do they, truth be told, think highly of Latour, he reads their letters with great pleasure whenever possible. And above all it pleases him to recall Uwe, "a giant and delicious German," an expert in silent hypnosis.

Mesmer's and Erickson's slow (he writes) *and somewhat ridiculous sessions, replete with repetitions and litanies, nurture clichés about hypnotism, but they are usually limited by language: few people are susceptible to falling into a deep trance, much less adapting to the violent ways of their hypnotist the way Latour likes, if the ritual doesn't rely on words from their mother tongue. And every verbally formatted attempt at suggestion may reveal to the victims, even if they are at an "unconscious level," the worst intentions of those who seek to exert control over them, with consequent, and sometimes invincible, reactions of rejection.*

Hence the usefulness of the absolutely original discipline advocated by Uwe, who replaces all verbal communication with direct violence. Strong and imposing, hardened by rigid workouts, Uwe stands before the subject and dominates him, introducing him into the rhythms of hypnosis through a four-stage strategy: confusion, panic, reduction to impotence, and surrender. The first blows, without any audible threat and delivered barehanded, are inflicted with moderate force to specific nerve endings: above all, they incapacitate the limbs. Then come other attacks, progressively more vigorous and painful, against which the victim cannot defend himself and which, in addition to inflicting terror, cause him to lose all clear perception of his surroundings amidst an infliction of suffering that isn't only constant but extended literally along the entire body. Then the pains begin to develop an order, traveling along the flesh in increasingly clear patterns, and then the latter grow more complex and develop into a source of irresistible attention, which ultimately satiates the victim's conscience. Just at the moment when the saturation of sensations renders the perception of greater suffering impossible, the victim has lost all control and his body has become manageable: he'll assume positions and integrate pre-established movements, all without Uwe having uttered a single syllable.

Latour thinks about Mundo, about the earliest moments of their relationship, and remembers his bewildered face, so often and so full of genuine stupidity.

41

"Something else I must point out is that he's crazy about me."

"I don't understand."

"Watch," Latour says, and shows Mundo a pornographic magazine opened to the middle page: a violent and complicated intercourse scene between six or seven men and women. Mundo ignores it: instead he looks at the other men at the party or at the floor. Latour's interlocutor still doesn't understand. Latour barely touches the base of Mundo's spine, and he turns to look at him, begins to pant, falls to his knees, begins to shake, gets up, touches himself with both hands, then holds them out in order to touch his master. He also sticks out his tongue and, with proper discretion, anyone is able to see how excited he is. But suddenly, when he is finally about to make contact, he stops, as if an invisible force were protecting Latour's body. Several attempts by Mundo—not only with his hands, but also with his torso and mouth—are similarly futile, and finally, while continuing to lunge against the nonexistent barrier, sweating, his eyes bulging, he begins to cry, one might say, out of frustration.

42

Karinna summarizes, beginning with her name, long traditions of vulgar taste, which is the only kind learned by millions and millions of people in the world (Latour writes). But when, as in Latour's case, it's a question of one option among many, everything in Karinna that is grotesque, disproportionate, and base becomes a series of supremely delightful attributes. A black albino, with huge breasts and ass, she was freed from one of the world's most refined and secret brothels. Ugly, grotesquely ugly, with coarse, uneven, and abrupt features, she was able to rid herself of her masters upon discovering that, the more she tried to hide her disproportion, the more it exalted her, and that in this exaltation there was an inexhaustible source of sexual attractiveness.

Now, Karinna, who isn't in particularly good shape or athletic, is equipped with one hundred eleven tattoos and a similar number of piercings distributed symmetrically on her body. The piercings are made with rings, nails, and several other rarely discreet objects—the four rings in her vaginal labia, for example, create a bulge in her very tight clothes—and the tattoos, although a careful inspection demonstrates the care with which they are done, give the initial impression of having been done in prison with a sewing needle, pen ink, and the letters (and spelling) of a functional illiterate. Cheap and brightly-colored fabrics, plastic and fake metal accessories, garish hairstyles and makeup complete her attire. She's a doll made by the hand of an idiot, smelling of polyester and sweat-soaked rubber. That anyone is attracted to her is a paradox that feeds on itself and grows increasingly more intense as the encounters grow longer, as Karinna adds her physical appearance to her long list of pain and pleasure techniques. Her apprenticeship in these techniques caused Karinna, in her day, to take much longer than she had anticipated to prepare and complete the image that she sought to create for herself. When she finished, however, she was able to make herself known almost immediately as an independent domme, almost nauseating to the eyes but at the same time irresistible. Only one of the specialists whom Latour frequents (to use their services and learn from them) charges higher rates.

Latour pauses. Mundo is asleep on a rug on the floor. He continues: *Disoriented, his memory partially blocked through the judicious use of certain substances—and after Uwe's first violations, which left him exhausted—Mundo thought he was just beginning his treatment when he was left with Karinna. He also believed that he could be saved if only he demonstrated himself to possess a greater moral stature than his captors: if he didn't surrender to Karinna's love, if he demonstrated that the values in which he professed to believe and the virtues he claimed to defend were able to withstand, effectively, all the attempts of perversion to which he would be subjected.*

Of course, Mundo didn't withstand, and in the span of some few days—aided only by additional small doses of the substances to which he had been subjected from the beginning, administered in his meals or during periods of sleep, so that he wouldn't be able to handle the unreality of his predicament—he swore to Karinna that he would do whatever she ordered him to do, that he would accept everything he was told, that he would leave everything, etc. The true vulgarity lay in the honesty of his submission and, above all, in the disgust and contempt for himself that were perceptible in every one of his words.

In memory of his fall, in no way clearer in his memory than in anyone else's, Mundo has a tattooed chain around his left heel and another real one, consisting of four rings driven into his flesh, around his right heel.

If someone had seen the car, slowly circling the outskirts of the city, they would have thought there was no one with Latour: Latour looking out the windshield, Latour clutching the steering wheel, Latour taking his hand away while the car braked abruptly and started moving again, to the bewilderment of his escorts.

A secondary area of Latour's knowledge is pornographers, which shouldn't be confused with fans of pornography, not even with amateur filmmakers: a certain minimal effort is required, if not to take pictures or films or to write stories, to sell them. Latour despises most of these entrepreneurs, small merchants without taste or talent who, what's more, give their work to distributors and middlemen; but as he, according to what he's been told, has investments in the trade, he finds it interesting to mix with them from time to time, go to their meetings, even invite them to one of his less ostentatious homes.

During one of these gatherings, Latour talked about free will with a producer of children's films:

"They don't think it's bad," he said. "I've asked them, and they don't tell me it's a sin, or that they're being abused."

"Really?" Latour asked in turn.

And the man smiled.

"What if I tell you that they all come from worse situations...? It's not really true, I don't know, well, of course it's not a criterion that I use to select them... but, look, what about your ...?"

"It's totally different," Latour replied, making a precise signal with his fingers in front of Mundo's eyes, who was wearing a pink rubber suit.

"It's totally different," Mundo repeated, standing up and extending his hand to the producer. "Totally different, because what exists between the master and me is, to a great extent, a gentlemen's agreement." The entire speech lasted a quarter of an hour and included many complicated paragraphs, filled with quotes and subordinate clauses. Latour smiled when his pet finished speaking without making a single mistake: it had taken him a great deal of work for Mundo to learn each word.

45

The collar closes around Mundo's neck, who now, for the first time, perceive the emptiness that precedes suffocation: his chest wants to move, his lungs inhale, but Latour keeps squeezing and, of course, is sitting on top of his body, dominating him with his weight. Mundo only has the right hand free, with which Latour doesn't engage so that his slave can write his impressions. Latour has placed a keyboard in front of him, on the rug, just at the limit of his reach.

Obedient, trembling, Mundo's fingers approach the white keys. They press the *I*, the spacebar, the *a* again, the *m*, the spacebar...

But it's not just that the effort required becomes greater every time; Mundo can't see the computer screen, which is in its place on the desk, more than a meter above his eyes, so he can't be sure that he's not made a mistake already, on one letter or all of them: maybe their relationship is already unintelligible, exactly like the thought that becomes diluted in agony or delirium. Worse yet, he can barely see the keyboard itself, as his arm, extended forward, covers almost half of his field of vision. And, so, Mundo is at constant risk not only of making a mistake, not only of not finishing, but of losing the use of the keyboard entirely, of being left without a voice ahead of his expected death: sometimes, if one of his movements becomes confused with a spasm or a tremor of panic, instead of his fingers hitting the keys they pound the edge of the keyboard, with the ensuing risk that the latter will slip away to a position too remote for his hand to reach.

He gasps once, then twice, while Latour strives to observe how much he can see of his twitching expression, of his increasingly violent movements, with only the shortest moments to glance at the clock.

46

Sometimes, Mundo puts on a white apron and a little cap (and absolutely nothing else) to act as Latour's maid. He then goes around the house, feather duster in hand, cleaning the most fragile objects and dusting the surfaces. He sings the latest hits or lets out long sighs. Latour sometimes orders this performance during a moment of boredom, or to impress a guest. But this particular show of humiliation doesn't excite him: it's one of many "charms" that Mundo has learned in this life of his.

47

Occasionally, once he finishes with Mundo and has asked that he be fetched, Latour is left alone in the torture room, where he examines the various devices—several of which are valuable antiques—he's acquired at great expense; they're all maintained in perfect condition and ready to be used as soon as their owner so orders.

Latour and Mundo spend long sessions with the wheels and pikes, the shackles and weights and locks. Every week they use a different device, according to a preestablished and strict order.

And because Latour has taken to writing here, and its atmosphere shouldn't be disturbed, there sits in a corner a wooden table from the seventeenth or eighteenth century, always stocked with handmade paper, metal inkwells, and authentic goose quills. Today, after noticing two drops of dried blood on a steel link, Latour promises to reprimand harshly those in charge of cleaning. Then he sits and takes out a blank sheet.

From the arrogance that affords him his position of privilege, Latour has on numerous occasions taken advantage of others' efforts not only without paying for it, but by denying any recognition of their contribution (Latour writes). *In this way he's indistinguishable from millions of people, equally exalted and miserable. Nor is he distinguished by the capriciousness of his gratitude, the tenacity of his hatred, the persistence of his vanities, the notion that the world could exist only as complement to his own existence; the appreciation of such sovereign and stupid freedom.*

48

Mundo watches television. This room, which Latour assigns him sometimes when he decides to have him inside the house, could have been a study once upon a time, or a bedroom.

However, in addition to the pallet on which Mundo sleeps, the two bowls for food and water, and of the pile of sawdust and paper that's changed with relative frequency, there's nothing except the huge screen, which is always on and projects, at full volume, an endless series of "indoctrination images": very fast shots of various objects, faces, of bodies in motion, to the rhythm of a pulsating and monotonous music, almost devoid of melody.

Before, long before, Mundo had to watch the images while lashed to a special chair, whose base is still screwed to the ground. Now, that he doesn't require any coercion to stay in the house with Latour, the chair isn't there and Mundo is subjected to the images only occasionally; then he squats and watches them, while striving to suppress any fleeting thought that doesn't precisely repeat what he sees and hears. Occasionally, he wants to find the word "Latour" or other keys ("love," "obedience," "pleasure") that are, according to what he was told at one time, hidden in the soundtrack. He's never heard them, he thinks, but even this thought must be repressed, while the music and images persist.

49

"Mundo wants, Mundo wants," Mundo justifies, aloud, while still trying to do a handstand in the garden. He takes a running start, launches forward, raises his feet, and falls. Every time. He tries again, because Mundo knows how to obey, even if Latour isn't there to see his progress.

50

Once, Latour agreed to receive some people who had been sent from a nearby city; their purpose was to examine him, to determine if he was well. Latour doesn't usually receive anyone he hasn't invited, and his "normal" servants, who exist in an imprecise but considerable number, know they shouldn't get in his way unless they're expressly called. But Latour answered the visitors' questions, allowed them to take blood and urine samples; he read letters printed on a sign; he listened to advice on health, feeding, and other issues. Latour couldn't remember the name of the person who had sent him the entourage, but he was affable and cooperative until the end. Then, because he had nothing to fear from them and because (he suddenly understood) he had wanted to do something similar for a long time, he called Mundo and displayed him, forcing him to do a few simple feats and other more difficult and painful ones. The faces of his visitors entertained him for a while. Then he ordered Mundo to imitate an attack dog and climb atop a fat nurse, to bite her neck, and cover her chest with saliva.

51

"If you want, I'll sell him to you."

"Sell him to me?"

"No, don't sell me. And don't you buy me. Don't buy me. Don't buy me. Don't buy me. Don't buy me. Don't buy me. Don't buy me." Mundo ends screaming, hugging the woman's legs, who's unable to free herself, while Latour has already begun to talk to someone else.

Of course, he and all the other guests—including those who are strolling in the garden or relaxing around the pool—are able to hear his screams clearly. Latour looks around and smiles: he's able to see some confused, or horrified, faces, and also the obvious effort of both men and women to hide their reactions, so as not to offend the owner of the home.

52

Of opaque voice and gestures, of medium height and complexion, his face is like anyone's. The rarity of Dr. Hertz, then, lies only in his name, trivial by virtue of sounding like certain other names or kinds of vulgar knowledge. It is precisely the oddity that fits someone like him, whose field of work is so precise and so politically incorrect: if he isn't known, he'll be remembered for his unusual surname more than the vagueness of his explanations and his accomplishments.

Dr. Hertz, at least, is indispensable to Latour. Mundo's cosmetic modifications, like the ones of those who have preceded him, do not pose problems: if they are necessary to combat boredom, any moderately capable maid or stylist can shave or dye hair, apply make-up and paints, insert and extract accessories, et cetera; on the other hand, no matter how exciting "pure violence," "clamps and razors," "tearing flesh without remorse," all these images, may be, Latour doesn't possess the necessary knowledge, nor could he acquire it without an effort that, in reality, he doesn't wish to exert.

Of course, what Latour allowed himself—as he has always allowed himself—was to begin Mundo's treatment with Dr. Hertz's operation, and with no preparation other than notice of what would happen. Bound in the trunk of the car, gagged, and blindfolded, Mundo could only hear the voice of his master, who introduced himself as such and who, from outside, explained to him the analogy between his case and that of domestic cats, and especially males.

"It's nothing against the cat," he said, "it's not a desire to harm it, it's not even the desire that it not have kittens. I love kittens. But if they are not treated, cats commit all sorts of outrages, they fight, they try to escape... And they live shorter lives. In reality, it's for their sake. The neutered cat is happier."

After these words, two of Latour's employees gave him time to withdraw and opened the trunk to give Mundo a few blows and administer a mild and rapid dose of anesthetic. When he left the operating room, Mundo awoke. They carried him on a stretcher; he had no idea that what he feared had happened to him, so he turned to Latour and begged him. In response, Latour ordered the stretcher to stop, removed the sheet that covered his victim's body and explained to him, in detail and without stopping amid the crying and shaking, the precise nature of the change.

Latour writes this, on a boring afternoon, while Mundo wallows inside a bathtub filled with chocolate syrup. Suddenly, Latour has the impression that he has wasted the syrup: he's not in the mood.

53

There are at least three lies in what has been said until now: Latour's writings aren't as extensive, copious, or eloquent as suggested so far, his habits aren't exactly as they have been described and, above all, Mundo isn't a victim of treatment or torture decided by others.

It is true, on the other hand, that Mundo has been trained to perform numerous routines and can react automatically, without any intervening reason or fear, to numerous stimuli. One of the most interesting is presented in the middle of the next scene, which Latour took a long time to concoct and teach him but which is among the most striking of the common repertoire:

When he wants to (almost always early in the morning, although sometimes at other times), Latour goes to look for Mundo wherever he is, puts on his leash, and takes him to one of the studios. Nothing can be heard, of course, as they both advance, and just as Latour doesn't speak, Mundo doesn't either, knowing what will happen and excited from the knowledge of the task to come: a clear affirmation of his devotion and obedience.

On the desk, next to the computer and phone, is the envelope, and inside the envelope a card with the woman's phone number. If there is no envelope, it means that the woman changed her residence or number, and it will be necessary to wait for the detective to locate her again. But this has become more and more rare over the years: the woman has learned that she'll always be found, because Latour is powerful—although she, of course, doesn't know Latour's name or have the slightest idea about his activities or his intentions—and, in addition, there's the mother-in-law anecdote. (For a while, the woman refused to have a phone, so Latour decided to tend to, instead, the woman's mother. The old woman, who was the mother, continued to be barraged with calls until the woman agreed to leave her hideout, visit her mother, answer the phone, beg through the receiver, and ensure that she would be available.)

Latour dials the number. Mundo waits. Latour waits for the first ring and connects the speaker of the phone, so that the two can hear and speak if necessary. It's dawn, so, as usual, the woman answers. (At other times the daughter answers, or the youngest son, but this, as has been said, is less common.) Then Latour says:

"Here, they want to talk to you."

And—as his master walks away to let him pass—Mundo, who recognizes the words as one of several preestablished keys, speaks articulately and clearly to say:

"Darling, it's me."

"Fernando," says the woman, whose name is Andrea; at one time it was a question, but she is no longer unsure and is resigned only to continue.

"Honey, I'm fine. I've been kidnapped. They took me, I don't know where I am, they want money. They want a million," Mundo says. "They say that if you don't give it to them they'll kill me. They say that if you give it to them tomorrow, you can have me back." Mundo's voice is devoid of any hint of anguish or fear. It's been years, no doubt, since Andrea believed in the possibility of his return, and even he doesn't want to go back. But what's important isn't their desires but proper obedience instead. If Latour's introductory words had been different, Mundo would have babbled like a child or barked like a dog; he would have feigned an affected tone, he would have put his butt and not his mouth next to the microphone, or he would have insulted the woman, called her a whore and frigid, cow, perra: the precise sequence of words that Latour indicated.

In this case, however, after "you can have me back," there's little left to say: a pair of protestations of love, a question about the welfare of their daughter and the baby (the lines haven't changed, it is understood that, during all this time, Latour has had Mundo) and a brief assurance that everything will be okay:

"We'll see each other tomorrow, darling. Right?" after which Latour, who invariably grows excited with the exchange, hangs up the phone, pulls down his pants and penetrates Mundo quickly, nervously.

"Okay," he says, several times, following his own rhythm. "Okay, okay." 田

Years Later

Like all the houses that go up in the barranca, a cable runs from this house to one of the light poles on the avenue. But it's broken again. If anyone came in now, they wouldn't see them. But no one's going to come in.

Outside you can hear the usual sounds at this time of the night: the voices of drunks, old men snoring, the yelling in the distance, the TVs, the electronic devices that belong to those who do have electricity, the water running at the bottom of the barranca. You can also smell the water, which runs from the houses and falls into shoddily excavated crevices and segments of pipe. The stench, nobody knows why, seems to come from below: it climbs through weeds and stones, passes through the gaps in the pieces of cardboard and laminate, filling all the spaces. Fires don't burn it; the wind—which every day blows in the garbage from the avenue, and which every so often leaves a house without a roof—doesn't carry it away.

A year ago, he saw, for the first time, the large hole in the wire mesh that encloses the property and the slope that comes out of the hole, that twists sharply to hug the hillside and turns into a path that becomes lost among the houses, looking downward, and reaches the bottom, a couple hundred meters farther down, where the construction ends and the cemetery begins.

"We can't get through down there?" he asked his companion.

"No mames," he said, adjusting his cap. "How are we going to get through? They carry their garbage through there," but he didn't point anywhere, and instead he started to walk again, pushing his trash bin on wheels.

Now, in the cold, narrow stretch between two houses, lies a dog, with several holes in its belly, at edge of a puddle, the water mingling with the blood. The children who did the killing surround it, holding their weapons. Everyone struggles to hear, between the rumble of other music, a cumbia that someone is playing at full volume somewhere in the distance, perhaps at a real dance in one of the surrounding colonias.

A few hours ago, she asked:

"Will you have a lot to do?" Her voice, as usual, sounded fatigued, as if she were talking in her sleep. The two crossed the avenue in the direction of the ravine. They could now see the corrugated roofs of the first houses; by walking past the sidewalk, they'd soon see the others and even the cemetery.

"What?" he answered, putting his hand to his ear.

"Do you have something to do," she said. They stopped in front of a makeshift stand. The woman who was helping him was readying the camping stove to cook and took out the plastic jar where she kept the oil. The liquid, he thought, shouldn't be more than a few days old: it had already turned gray, but it was still transparent and almost nothing was floating in it. The woman poured it onto the surface of the comal, and both saw it suddenly heat up and start to boil.

"No," he said, "I'm done for today," and he showed her his empty hands. He had just left his broom along with the others in the warehouse.

She didn't understand the gesture but said nothing.

"And you?" he asked.

He had to repeat it because a pair of trucks with double trailers roared past them. The woman with the comal was preparing cheese tacos and threw them in the boiling oil.

Now, the woman is frying potato tacos in the same oil: she takes some mashed potato from a plastic bowl, puts it on the tor-

64

tilla, rolls it up, and secures it with a toothpick. The oil has turned black but customers—a taxi driver, a couple of prostitutes, a vagrant with a bit of luck—are waiting anxiously.

And he, inside the tiny house, hasn't taken off his orange coveralls, covered in thick stains, but she hugs him anyway, takes him by the face, kisses him with the same false moan that she dedicates to others, which she's unable to contain.

A while ago, he went to the corner where she works, on the other side of the avenue, where the overpasses lead to the abandoned warehouses, with walls covered in graffiti. The cars park in a hurry, picking up whoever's waiting then leaving. She was arguing with her pimp, who started to hit her. He waited until the pimp finished and left, then approached her.

"How much?" he asked.

"What?" she answered. She was still on the ground.

"How much?"

"No, not right now. Can't you see?"

He knelt and looked straight into her eyes.

"Please, get up," he said. She managed to stand, with difficulty, but he remained on his knees.

Many times, after that first night, he's gotten in the same position. And she, whenever she sees him do it, feels the same impulse.

"Don't laugh," he tells her, but doesn't stand up.

Then she found out that, before meeting her, he had knelt before lots of other people from the colonia, and he still does it, sometimes to make a humble request—as if to say "please" with all his body—and others for reasons less clear. But now, as they kiss, she doesn't think about that. She tries to focus on the moment. Only occasionally, she's distracted by the screams of a baby and its mother in a nearby house. The mother, who yells again and again at the baby to shut up, has (as expected) a much stronger voice, and so it continues, to the point that sometimes you can't hear the baby at all, just the screams of the mother. It's rare that the television, which is always on (this house has better electrical wiring, because it has its own cable), can be heard more clearly than the voices.

"He's crazy," her friend Vecky told her, after seeing them together for the first time.

"What do you mean crazy?"

"No mames. He's always on his knees."

"It isn't all the time."

"And he talks to himself."

"So?"

"Well, look at you. Just don't start giving him a discount because..."

She didn't finish, but she didn't say anything else: she just continued to look at her.

He fumbles to caress her, clumsily: his hands stumble again and again against the swollen flesh of her sides, her stomach and butt, which yields to the pressure but not immediately. The contact always reminds him how the sides of any garment she wears are deformed. Now he touches her breasts, enormous and heavy; as always, he dislikes the contact. But imagining the contact was what caught his attention when he saw her for the first time, standing on his sidewalk, wearing only a short skirt, a sleeveless shirt, and black high heels. Her hair wasn't only pulled back in a very tight ponytail, which didn't hide any part of her face. What's more, her hands were interlocked on the back of her neck, and every so often, without warning, she'd throw the elbows back, so that her chest would stick out.

"So, Chief, you mean you still... at your age...?" asked his boss yesterday, who assigns him the streets he's to sweep, records his attendance, and pays him every two weeks.

"At my age what?" he asked in turn.

"Don't be offended. Me, when... when I'm as old as you, I hope I'm still..."

"Oh, no, what do you mean, at my age... A man's already tuckered out."

His boss laughed.

"The truth is nothing stands up and everything hangs down, as we disgust everyone. I know I stink worse when I don't wear the uniform. People tell me: "Chale, pinche ruco, they oughta take you and your trash and burn you with it or somethin' so that you don't ruin the city, because you offend me. You're botherin' me. You hear me, puto? You offend me, and it's a waste that you're even still alive, breathing air that I could be breathing, and just for that this pinche city's disgusting, you..."

He raised his arms, clenched his teeth, strutted through the office. Other people stopped to watch.

Over the years, after his arrival at the barranca, the neighbors had brought sandbags and debris to reinforce the foundation of the houses, built using even more fragile materials, and also to reduce the slant of the slope. Doing it was indispensable: on both sides of the cemetery are the remains, worn and almost unrecognizable, of many houses that the landslides ripped out or that simply collapsed where they were. She told him this story, one night, while the two lay in the cot that occupies half the space of the house. She didn't tell him if she had been among those first occupants of the barranca. And she doesn't say anything as she unzips his coveralls, and he, in turn, begins to pull down her skirt. Instead, she moans once or twice. When her skirt has fallen to the floor, he fumbles to take off her shoes. She allows him, but, as soon as he finishes, she quickly removes his coveralls and lays them on the cot. Then she mounts him.

"I'm glad you finally decided to come," he says.

She's never seen another body with so many scars, so ravaged: his back is covered with furrows and holes, and his belly, at once swollen and full of wrinkles, and not uniformly white, as she expected: on the contrary, it's covered in brown, gray, green spots, whose origin is unknown. In addition, his navel has a metal ring, partially buried in a flowering of flesh but still visible.

"A long time ago," he explained, the first time she saw him naked. "It looked better before but it got infected."

Now, after kissing the ring, she also kisses his pelvic bones, which protrude and tighten the skin; his sleeping member between his legs, under a sparse, black forest, and the scars on his thighs and heels.

A few months ago, just after he decided to move out of the room where he lived, the two got drunk on a couple of bottles, full and unopened, that he found in his bin. He'd never found anything like it, and the two thought it was appropriate to celebrate. Since the house had electric light, he waited for her on the cot and watched television. When she returned, the two began to serve each other in plastic cups: they didn't know exactly what they were drinking, but it tasted good—it was probably some fruit liqueur, maybe even the kind made at home—and soon they were laughing and kissing. They made love a couple of times and fell asleep until the next morning.

Vecky came to wake them up.

"Where were you?" she asked. "You know who's really pissed off. You had people waiting."

He also missed work. While he went to save his job, she went to receive a beating. When they met again he took her to the nearest pharmacy, on the other side of the overpasses, to buy gauze and alcohol. Then they took the wrong microbus to go back and, lost in a colonia they didn't know, walked a couple of kilometers until they arrived back at the avenue.

They went into a tiny fonda to eat, which they had never seen. There was nothing but bread and coffee. The two were halfway through when a man came up to their table and sat down.

"This is a kidnapping," he told them. He was bald, he didn't have eyebrows or eyelashes, and his hands trembled. I'm going to steal some of your time because I want to show you, make you partakers of my work. I am Abdalá Martínez de las Fuentes, and I've had a literary career for twenty-seven years, independent, without depending on anyone and without ever having copyrighted a single one of my poems, because I think art belongs to everyone. If you'll allow me, I would like to read. I have several, several copies too..."

The stranger opened a portfolio he was carrying and took out a mass of photocopies clipped together. He separated them and went about showing them. There were numerous sets of poems. The couple read some titles quickly.

"Which one do you like? Choose one. That one?" She made a vague gesture in the direction of one of the sheets. "Very well. I'll read them to you. I hope you enjoy them."

Sr. Martínez read:

BORN A SLAVE
(For Ma. Luisa Cervantes)

"As you can see" he clarified "it is dedicated, but I'll forego the information in the dedication, because this reflection I consider to be universal."

"Ah," she said.

And Sr. Martinez began again:

BORN A SLAVE
(For Ma. Luisa Cervantes)

Attach the body
always to what the spirit orders
if you don't want to live everything
without taking advantage of nothing

'tis better you leave that life
that torments you now
and live anew hour after hour
so that it is not a lost life!
knowing that of your creator
you are only a slave

but a slave born
of God: you are that kind of slave!

thus you will understand... the essence
of your being and you will not regret
surrendering to the power that is more
benevolent and more virtuous!

and you will know that your rebel being
was inexperienced at an early age
and that true freedom...
lies forever in following it!

"I," Señor Martínez continued, "am called Abdalá, which means 'servant of God,' and this poem has become my autobiography. But it also has a message, which is symbolized in poetry verses. For example, in the first stanza is the rhyme, which I did well by making it rhyme not in the classic style but rather in opposite lines. Contradictory. You noticed, right? Body and spirit, everything and nothing, are the key words key to understanding..."

Since then he's not been back to the fonda: in part, according to what he's said, because of the words he had said to Sr. Martínez before he could continue:

"I don't give a shit about poetry."

Sr. Martínez stopped suddenly, blinked several times, and raised a trembling finger as he said:

"I don't see, señor, any reason for you to speak to me in that tone and in front of the señorita."

"She's not a señorita."

"In front of the señora who deserves respect," Sr. Martínez said.

"Yes, of course, respect," he replied, and so on for a very long while, during which everyone present heard the increasingly strident refutation of all the ideas that Sr. Martínez dared to formulate.

Now she says:

"Wait," and she gets off the cot. She walks to the wooden table, taken from a dump, at the end where the hotplate sits. Under the other end is a box, which she bends over to pick up. In doing so, she hits herself on the edge of the table but doesn't say anything.

There's only one house below than theirs, closer to the cemetery. And inside, right at that moment—by a chance that neither of them will ever know—several hands lift from the dirt floor an extremely heavy bundle, made of half-rotted blankets. A death rattle is coming out of the bundle but nobody hears it.

He also doesn't know that she's returned many times to the fonda to eat and, although she's not run into Sr. Martínez again, she has become friends with the cook, who from the first day insisted on speaking to her. The cook belongs to a cult that demands that its faithful constantly seek new followers, and she fulfills that obligation; she's not managed to convince her to come to her temple, but neither has she given up, and today—given that she already knows some details from her past—she tried a new strategy: to make her believe that her life is terrible and that she deserves something better.

"*Someone* better," she stressed, "someone who really loves you."

"I'm an ass," she replied, "and he's a cock. It's that simple. Why can't people understand that?"

The cook opened her mouth.

"For that matter, it's even simpler: I'm an ass and so is he."

Now she's opened the box and removed the object. It has two tips and both seem clean but in reality, in addition to being very worn, they have tiny remnants of dirt, hardened, now impossible to remove. For a long time, neither she nor he has cared to clean them thoroughly.

She takes the object to him. He touches it, to get his bearings in the dark, and brings his nose to one of the tips. Almost immediately he half-opens his lips. She doesn't see it. Instead, she thinks of the object itself: the cardinal number of the occasions in which she has used, felt, the object. She has no idea what it could be. Since the last day, when she left the other house, she has carried that relic with her.

He says:

"Now?"

She doesn't answer. He gets on all fours and lifts his butt without getting off the cot, to offer the best possible angle. He then closes his eyes, although there's still no light and all he can perceive is contact from one of her hands, which creeps up his thighs and gropes for the canal. He then feels the tip. Then the rest. She moves toward the other end of the object, certain, while a car drives slowly down the avenue, far above them and above everyone. ⏃

b)

I always say, tomorrow...
and then forget. And proudly show company
a room that shines with the golden rule
my mother gave me.

Rosario Castellanos

54

"Güey, pinche Rodrigo..."

"Didn't I tell ya to wait for me outside."

"But I gotta..."

"Give 'im a bump so he won't be fuckin' with us, pinche Rodrigo," said the actor. "I'm gonna lose my hard-on."

"Go away," Rodrigo said. "Didn't you fuckin' hear, pinche Marlene? Get out, ¡chingada madre, hija de tu puta...!

He didn't stop the recording when he got up, and the camera was able to record how the actor pulled out of the actress. It didn't see, however, how Rodrigo went over to Marlene and hit her hard on the top of the head: bam!, with an open hand, to humiliate her. Nor did it see how she didn't back down but, on the contrary, began to wrestle with him, resisting his efforts to force her out of the room and speaking in a low voice, quickly, so that no one could hear her between Rodrigo's screams and the noise their bodies made as they banged against the walls and furniture. Only when they both hit the camera itself did they appear on the tape, going in and out of the frame, jerking back and forth, indicating that the device was about to fall until the hand of one of those present (no one knows who) stopped it. Finally, Marlene was able to get close enough to murmur, in Rodrigo's ear, seven words. The movement, and her own face, remain in the center of the shot, along with Rodrigo's head and a bare window that looks onto a brick wall.

You can also clearly see how the man turned away sharply and opted this time for a stronger blow: a backhand, from right to left, that threw her to the floor.

Instead of returning to the recording, however, he turned away from Marlene, pulled the tape out of the camera and left.

"I told you," the actress said, putting on her robe: "When you hang out with him, it's totally different."

"It pisses him off when he loses his... how do you say it?" the actor asked.

"Composure. But no, he's high as a kite."

"What do I do with the pinche camera?" one of the other guys said.

You could hear Rodrigo kicking the wall in the hallway from where they were.

"Hey, pinche Marlene, what did you say to him?"

Although what could be saved from the interrupted intercourse scene had been copied, the rest of the recording wasn't erased and still exists, stored at the house in the town, that Marlene abandoned many years later and that nobody has inhabited again.

Marlene had said:

"You're gonna be a dad, cabrón."

55

"You're always naked, aren't you?" the deputy director asked.

Yuyis didn't answer. She didn't know what to say.

"You're...?" the deputy director began, but gave up. He closed the door and began to loosen his tie.

56

When he decided that he could *never* sleep again: that the racket would go on and on and on and on and that nothing could be done, Marlene decided to accept her cousin's offer and talk to the police.

"Porn."

"And?"

"Plus, they stick things in themselves."

The policeman didn't say anything.

"Tell him the other thing," her cousin said.

"What thing?" Marlene asked.

"What thing?" the policeman asked.

Her cousin reminded her, quickly, and she said:

"Oh, that."

"Is it true?" the policeman asked.

"Yes, yes it's true."

"That's enough for us to bust 'em."

"It's just that they're really..." Marlene began, but couldn't find the right words and stopped. Her idea was to describe the recording sessions with the girls (as she referred to them) and also with the little boys. They all seemed bad to her: they didn't know how to act, and they weren't nice or anything: a lot of times they were horrible.

"The day you least expect it, they'll do the same to the baby girl too," the cousin interrupted. The baby, lying in an old crib in the next room, hadn't stopped crying.

57

Sometime later, now in the house that had belonged to her mother, Marlene looked at the little girl, who hadn't learned to walk but was now moving from one side to the other: she supported one arm on the floor and threw her legs forward. It reminded Marlene of a friend of hers, who when she was drunk wasn't able to get up and always crawled in the same way.

"Pinche Yuyis," she said, in a half-precarious smile. She realized she could only remember her friend's nickname.

58

From time to time, despite everything, she had taken the time to teach her a few words:

"Yuyis," she'd say as she waved a hand. The two of them watched TV. Yuyis had a chin full of food scraps, but Marlene was too comfortable to get up and give her a bath.

"Uyis," the girl would say, and she's shake weakly.

"No: Yuyis," Marlene said. "Yuuuu, yissss."

"Uyis."

"Ay, hija de tu pinche madre…"

"Che made," Yuyis said.

59

With the camera on and recording, Marlene approached the bed to watch Yuyis' performance. She felt restless.

"Yes, yes," Yuyis said, "Yes. More."

She didn't do it well: she said the words, moved her hips, she was breathing heavily, just as he had seen in so many movies, but something was missing. Something had always been missing.

"Oh, oh, oh," said the guy, who didn't do it well either but, apart from that, was just a poor idiot: the driver of one of the trucks that transported the films. His two companions, who carried the boxes and took care of the money, hadn't been able to get an erection and waited to the side, carefully out of the camera's field of vision.

"Hold on," Marlene said.

"I already came," the guy said.

Marlene never figured out how to describe or resolve the problem. In the morning, while alone at her desk, she consoled herself by imagining the best performances she knew how.

60

The object was called Dildo. She forgot about it later, but during that time, when Marlene wasn't there, Yuyis played with it: she'd take it and make it roll on the floor, like a little car. And, sometimes, she talked to it.

She believed that everyone in the world had names with two syllables: Yuyis, Marlene, Dildo… There was also Señor, who would sometimes come to the house and from whom she was supposed to hide really well, because he was bad and if he saw her, he was capable of taking her far away. Like Marlene, who from time to time, agreed to teach her some words, she played at teaching them to Dildo, and above all she took it upon herself to repeat the names to him. She didn't learn to say "mystery" until much later, while working on *The Mystery of the Hairy Cave*, but the term would have been useful to her in her lessons. She was fascinated by the mystery of the regularity of the names, their affinity with the beat of their own voice, and also the fracture: Marlene and Señor were different, fearsome, and maybe it was like that because their names were pronounced in another way: the opposite.

"It's not MAR-len," she'd teach Dildo. "It's Mar-LENE, Mar-LENE, Mar-LENE, Mar-LENE, Mar-LENE, Mar-LENE"—and in the end she'd march around the room, tottering or falling, which she never managed to stop completely, waving her baton to the sounds of those syllables that came out, too, with that strange movement of her tongue, which moved back and forth inside her mouth.

"Shut up, pinche Yuyis!" Marlene would say when she arrived and found her going in circles, around the dining room table or from one side of the hall to the other, feverishly, making Dildo go up and down.

61

"I mean, I didn't want to," she explained as she got up. She would've said more but it was hard for her to speak: her jaw didn't want to move.

It had already been made clear that she wasn't to be arrested, but the apartment was still full of police and photographers. Two of them had gotten their hands on photos of Marlene, but the others chose to concentrate on the shelves full of videos and, above all, the screen where she remained, motionless in the pause where Rodrigo had left it, the face of a boy in the middle of being fellated. The photos weren't for media the photographers collaborated with regularly, but rather to circulate in other ways. A photographer who was more daring than his colleagues grabbed a couple of tapes while no one was watching.

"So what the fuck did you want?" her cousin asked. "Sit down."
She didn't sit.

"Make him...," she said, "scared."

"No mames, Marlene. Sit down."

Marlene crouched down to search under bed.

"You knew," her cousin said. "You knew that if they came down on him..."

Marlene couldn't respond to that accusation and instead said:

"He wasn't... He wasn't coming back... He was going around with one of those... The one they took away just now. Did you see her? The one with the green hair? Besides. He said he wasn't the father. That he wasn't going to... Un hijo de la chingada. And me..., I said... I said why am I going to waste my time on a pendejo like..."

Rodrigo was editing the fellatio scene when the police arrived. His only mistake (but Marlene didn't understand this at the time) was that he was the newcomer: that he'd just moved to that part of the city, and that he didn't pay the necessary fees that would allow him to work. His cousin's friend was working in more established businesses, and so the idea of attacking Rodrigo, "a stranger," worked out.

"Well, he's really not coming back now," her cousin said. "You hear? And cover yourself up," he added, as he put a sheet on her back.

Marlene got up and the sheet fell to the floor. She went to the window, opened it, and started looking outside, underneath the sill.

"Get inside, Marlene, you're naked!"

"He was the one who told me... He told me not to have the...What do you call it? The D&C."

The cousin went to Marlene, pushed her away from the window, put the sheet back on her back and forced her to put on panties and some sandals.

"Wait. They'll be here..., at any moment they'll be here..."

"No, you wait," the cousin said. Listen to me... did you want to do it? Did you want..."

Rodrigo appeared on all the television newscasts as head of an international child pornography ring, with a monopoly in all the states in the center of the Republic and with distributors in eleven countries. He's still in jail. Like Marlene, almost all the adults on her usual team were able to escape and change jobs or start over with other distributors. Three of the children, including the one present on the screen, went to orphanages; the others were able to continue.

"They're gonna come and take everything," she said.

"What the hell, Marlene."

Marlene began to shake. She was very cold.

"Marlene, that's murder."

She went into the bathroom and examined the toilet. She was afraid to push down on the handle.

"You didn't see them take out... little sacks of nothing, right? Right now."

"Why do you fuck if you don't want to have children?"

"To eat, pendejo," she replied furiously, as the sheet fell from her back. In the makeshift crib in a dresser drawer, the baby girl began to cry. "But there it is, right? And I'm going to take responsibility, right? I'm not asking for your pinche help. I'm gonna set up my own business."

"What?"

The sheet fell back on the floor.

62

"You don't use...?"

"What do you mean, don't fuck with me," the deputy director said, but smiled. "Let's see your little toy... Is it really made of metal?"

"I dunno."

"Not a lot of men come through here, right?"

63

"No," Yuyis asked. "Stop."

"Wait."

"Pinche madre," but Marlene didn't stop. She pulled Yuyis' legs apart and, with very little struggle, was able to insert Dildo. Yuyis felt something expand inside her, and then said:

"Ay."

"I'm eight years and three months old, and..., not four months... I've been waiting *un chingo*...."

"Ay," Yuyis said again, because Marlene was pulling on Dildo and the feeling of emptiness, in that place she hadn't know about until not long before, had become strange.

"I've been waiting for *un chingo*," Marlene said again. She also put Dildo back in, and this time Yuyis realized that she felt pain. The toy was soft and smooth between the palms of her hands, and although it slid easily along the floor, it required force to insert it into her and felt like thousands of scratches all at once.

"¡Ay, pinche madre!"

"*Un chingo*," Marlene said again, and Dildo's second withdrawal was also painful, and the new entry was even more so, and it was a while before Yuyis began to feel some relief.

When she finished, Marlene said:

"Now you're going to pay. I don't know why I paid attention to your puto padre, but now you're going to pay."

It was a long time before Yuyis played with Dildo again, despite the fact that Marlene no longer hid it and kept it within view from then on.

64

"I'm going to buy you," Marlene said, "some cute dresses."

Yuyis, sitting in an armchair in the living room, scratched her groin.

"What?" She asked.

"Yes, absolutely, a bunch of dresses. Absolutely. Plus, I'm going to buy, what do you call 'em? Things, props, so things look better than just the curtains, right? So it looks better than just paint. What'd you think? Yes? Yes, right? It'd be pretty. The movies would be better. Maybe I'll even start to distribute them..."

Yuyis turned to look at her and recognized the nervous movement of her hands.

"Wipe your nose," she said.

"Oh!" Marlene complained. "Don't talk back. I mean, it was good for you too, wasn't it? Come with me."

Yuyis followed her.

"Can I put it there too?"

"As long as you like it down there," Marlene said as they entered the room.

65

"Just go," said Marlene, still looking at the television screen.

Yuyis didn't hear her because she was in the bathroom, but Marlene hadn't noticed.

"You're just like her. Identical," she continued, pointing to the girl who was telling her story on the show. "You could've been a performer."

66

"Eat it all."

"No."

"I want the plate clean, do you understand me?"

"Wash it. Lazy bitch. Do that at least."

"If you keep talking back to me..."

"What, *pendeja*?"

"Go on, Yuyis, do it."

"What, *puta*?"

"I'll take you out."

"Oh yeah, let's see you do it!"

"I'm gonna take you out."

"Take me out then."

"I'm gonna take you out!"

"What are you waiting for, pinche bruja?"

Almost nothing ever happened after these arguments. But that day Marlene got fed up, jumped on Yuyis and picked her up really high. Yuyis twisted and managed to kick her in the face with one foot, but Marlene didn't let her go; she walked to the patio door, opened it, and threw Yuyis out, who fell face down on the dirt ground.

Stunned, Yuyis looked up to realize that it was already pitch dark. Marlene dropped the plate with the remainder of her dinner on her: she felt the blow of the plastic on her back and then the moisture of the pieces of meat and broth, which dribbled down her belly.

For the first few hours (this, Marlene observed, was something new: it was pride) she refused to say anything, but around two or three in the morning she was already moaning and complaining as usual. She'd hit the door with her palms or her head, and from the window you could see that she was still spread out, sometimes curled up and at time with her legs stretched out. She was trying, Marlene knew, to keep anyone from knowing she was there.

Yuyis was afraid that they would come for her. Suddenly, after a long wait, in the distance you could hear an indecipherable noise: perhaps someone in the town was shouting, an object making its way through the desert blown by the wind, an animal scratching on rocks; then she changed position. She didn't know which one would make her less visible: at time she tried to lay flat, put as much as her body close to the ground as possible, and at others she squeezed her body tight, to take up less room.

Once or twice, the sound of a car engine could be heard far away, and Yuyis began to squirm on the ground, frantic, like a fish in its last moments.

The next morning, tired, rubbing her eyes, Marlene finally opened the door. Yuyis had fallen asleep there, on the ground, despite the cold and the roughness of the stones among the tamped-down earth.

"What's your name?"

"Juan," the deputy director said. "Is your name really 'Yuyis'?"

"Yes, why?"

"What's your last name?"

"My what?"

Yuyis was ten years old when Marlene read the news in a paper: a woman had been arrested for biting her months-old son to death. She didn't like "that he never shut up."

"Mamá," Yuyis shouted, lying on the patio.

Marlene was surprised that she used that word: she'd not been speaking more or less that well for very long, and she'd never taught her that term or anything like it.

"Don't let them take me away, Mami," Yuyis pleaded, "don't let them take me away."

With that second surprise, Marlene completely forgot the feeling of shock that the story of the homicidal mother had caused her, considering she'd been punishing Yuyis in the same way for a long time, and not always at night, in reality whenever no one could see her.

Besides the house, Marlene had inherited from her mother a secretarial position: she had the right to go to the building, sit at a desk, and receive a salary with certain perks. Since there was almost never anything else to do other than preparing official documents and other similar tasks, Marlene could have spent a lot of time on each of them, so that they would last the entire day. On the contrary, however, she liked to finish in a hurry (but not submit them in a hurry, so she didn't look bad to her coworkers) and use her free time to devote to her own matters.

The most urgent of these had to do with her business, but none was too demanding: the truck arrived every fifteen days, every other Thursday at three in the morning, and all she needed to do was confirm the arrival a day or two in advance; the smaller trucks, vans, and foot messengers that collected the merchandise in order to distribute it throughout the state arrived with the same discretion and with the same low frequency; the hardest part was keeping Yuyis locked up.

So she was able to devote herself to her fantasies. Her desk was always in a hallway, in view of everyone, but Marlene knew to stay quiet behind a magazine, or by slowly eating a snack, while she fantasized.

70

"We did this once already," Yuyis said.

"So?"

"Don't you like it like this for a change?"

There was no response and Yuyis continued painting the fabric blue.

Marlene suddenly said:

"Or what, you don't like to play anymore?"

"No," Yuyis said, "I do."

"Okay, that's enough. Go to where I keep the cassettes and bring me one."

The first thing Marlene heard was the sound of the footsteps approaching the door, dotted with voices and clicks. Then the door boomed as it opened, as if it the army were arriving.

Marlene understood immediately, but her first clear thought was that she had never registered Yuyis and that doing so would have served, at least, to avoid various difficulties that she was now undoubtedly going to have.

Then it occurred to her that Yuyis herself might have numerous problems in her future life, and this thought surprised her: she had always thought she hated her. Between the banging and doors' opening, she began to hear shouting. An armed man appeared at the end of the hall. Marlene had time enough to think that perhaps she wasn't as bad a person as she had believed, and this idea comforted her.

"Let's see. So," the man said, "there are ten with women, four with gays, and one with an animal."

"And the one with kids," Marlene said, "there's a whole box of kids."

"They're video CDs," said the other man.

"And?"

"Now people want nothing but bootlegs."

"It's the same thing, Latour," Marlene replied.

"You can't tell them to record them on DVDs now?"

"As soon as I see them," Marlene assured him, without the slightest interest. It was hard enough for her to stay on good terms with the friends she'd left in the business.

Her clients usually came in the evening; the town was a long ways from her house, and to be honest there were never any curiosity seekers that ventured to a place where there were only, in addition to Marlene's own house, two or three others, all vacant and in ruins; there wasn't even a memory, among the people of the town, of the councilmen who had stolen so much money for so long and who, in the end, hadn't managed to finish the construction of those cold, gray monstrosities.

Their distributors left carrying the boxes, which would be sold in the surrounding municipalities. They never entered the next room, where Marlene kept her own movies.

73

In her fantasies Marlene punishes Yuyis, relentlessly, and the clearest and most obvious sign that her victim is defenseless is her nudity. Yuyis does the housework naked, eats naked, sleeps naked, waits for Marlene naked when she goes to work, naked she pleads with her to hit her, to not throw her out, to allow her make one more movie.

However, when Yuyis was four or five years old, Marlene came home from the office to find her covered with a sheet and, worse still, wearing one of her bras and panties tied in knots so that they would fit her body. It wasn't the first time it happened, and Yuyis justified what she had done just as she had other times:

"I'm cold," she said, but her tone was (Marlene perceived it clearly) defiant, like that of mean girls or women murderers on TV.

From then on, Marlene didn't force her to undress with the same insistence. Many nights she even allowed her to wear a sweater; once she even bought her a nightgown, although she changed her mind before giving it to her.

"Well, you don't fuck that bad."

Yuyis didn't answer.

"Say thank you."

"Thank you," Yuyis said.

The deputy director finished dressing. As he was knotting his tie, he suddenly stopped and sat down in the bed.

"Again?" she asked, and assumed a sensual pose, her eyes closed, mouth open, and knees bent, ready to open her legs when asked.

"No, no, wait. Listen. Tell me about yourself."

Yuyis opened her eyes.

"Do you work with Señora Marlene? You live here? Are you her relative?"

"I'm her daughter."

The deputy director was silent for a few moments.

"Tell me. Do a lot of people come to you?"

"What?"

"How many people do you fuck?"

"One at a time."

"No, how many other people does your mother bring here?"

"Just you."

The deputy director fell silent again. Yuyis thought she could caress him, but when she raised her hand, the man didn't even look at her. Yuyis kept her hand in the air.

"Do you know," the deputy director asked, still not looking at her, "that what she's doing to you is against the law?"

"What?"

"Are you an idiot?"

"Yes, señor, yes, señor, yes, señor," Yuyis said, as she lowered her hand and closed her eyes again.

"Yes, yes," said the actress in the movie.

"Yes, yes," said Yuyis.

"Again," Marlene ordered.

"Yes, yes," Yuyis said again. She was genuinely trying to imitate the voice she heard on the television. There were many months of training while Marlene recorded a series of tapes that she never wanted to see again.

"This is boring," Yuyis said.

"Keep doing it. Or do you want to go to school?"

"What?"

"Keep going and shut up. Or say something, then..." Marlene tried again to correct herself; she began to stutter, closed her fists, got up, and turned off the TV.

At night, when Marlene slept more soundly, Yuyis would get up, throw something on (the nights were cold year-round) and would go down to the living room, where there the television was. The idea had occurred to her, precisely, by watching a program in which a girl did the same. For the first two or three months, she watched the images without sound; little by little she dared to do more.

Over time, and with the help of the examples she saw on the available channels (she never put on training movies, as Marlene called them), she learned to read the numbers on the clock in order to know when she needed to go back to bed. She also learned to read some words: the names of singers and actors, those of some programs and brands. She wasn't able to make out the lyrics as clearly, and she was almost never curious about the long lists of names that could be found in the programs' credits or in the magazines that Marlene had left lying around the house.

She loved watching music videos with men and women who danced, moving their hips, always happy and sensual. When nobody was listening, she hummed the songs. Once a few notes slipped out in front of Marlene, and when she asked her:

"What is that?" she told her the name of the song and Marlene began to chat with her, without giving it a second thought. That night, after a long time of not using it, Marlene took Dildo out again.

77

Yuyis heard, as on other occasions, an argument between Marlene and the deputy director. He went into her room and did what he had come to do, but when it was over, like the time before, he lingered a moment.

"Hey, would you do me a favor?"

Yuyis thought she understood, but the deputy director stopped her from getting on her knees.

"No, wait, I'm serious... You know when the people in the movies come? Right? Look: we're going to fuck with your mother, and well I imagine you'd like us to fuck with her, right? Take this."

Yuyis held out her hand and recognized that the object was a cell phone.

"For me?"

"Yes, yes, for you. It is my birthday present."

Yuyis felt very moved, but the deputy director continued talking:

"When we end up with your pinche madre's business, I'm going to give you more presents. You understand me? But you have to help me."

"Pinche Yuyis," Marlene would say whenever she took off the diaper and discovered that her daughter had sores again. "Didn't I tell you to let me know."

"Pinche made," Yuyis would say, who preferred the pain of the sores than undergoing the treatment. She stirred and screamed as Marlene cleaned her and applied the alcohol. She had already spent most of the day locked up, but the town's climate is extreme: she was only comfortable in the summer months.

"Shut up, I'm your mother," Marlene would say, as she applied talcum powder.

"Pinche made," Yuyis repeated, occasionally kicking her hard enough to hurt her.

79

It was past midnight. To muster the courage, Yuyis played with Dildo, but at last she thought she couldn't wait any longer.

She took the cellphone from its hiding place, dialed the number that the deputy director gave her and, after listening to the ringtone a couple of times, she heard him say:

"It's like spies, cabrón, so now you want…" and an unknown voice said something that Yuyis couldn't understand. "Who is it?"

"Yuyis," she replied excitedly: she'd never called anyone.

"Are they on their way?"

"Who?"

"The movie people."

"Oh, yes, they're already here."

"Órale pues. I need you to leave for me right now."

"What?"

"Leave."

"Leave?"

"Unless you want them to put you in the slammer."

"What is that?"

"I tell you what, this girl has to be retarded," the deputy director said, and Yuyis understood that he wasn't talking to her. "Pay attention. Get out of your house now. Get out and start running straight this way."

"Where to?"

"Tell her I'll give her a job," the other voice said.

"Shut up. Look, girl, you have to leave and come here... to the City Hall building... because if you don't you're going to be fucked," and hung up.

Yuyis spent a long time without moving, sitting in her room, shaking. All of a sudden, she didn't know what to do. She didn't know what the City Hall was or where it was. And the deputy director had never told her that anything could happen to her when they did to Marlene what they were going to do.

Then she heard the engines as they approached: there were several, more fierce and powerful than she could have ever imagined, so she started to run, naked, with the cellphone in one hand and Dildo in the other, and she reached the door and felt the cold but didn't dare stop, and stumbled after a few steps, and the phone fell out of her hand, but she got back up, screaming in terror, and came to the highway and began to walk away, faster and faster, because it seemed like each of her screams belonged to someone else who was going to come after her.

80

"Run, güey," one of the guys from the truck yells, but the sound of his steps disappears in the commotion of everyone who's entered the house.

"Police," the agents shout, "police."

Marlene, in the kitchen doorway, wonders where Yuyis is. The first policeman can be seen at the end of the hallway. It looks like a scene from a movie: one of those eternal moments.

So as not to see the man anymore, Marlene raises a hand; she finds the switch and turns off the lights. ⌸

I was more romantic, perhaps, back when
I would scratch the stone
and I would say, for example, singing
from the shadow to the shadows,
astonished by my own silence,
for example, "it is time
to plow the winter,
and there are furrows and men in the snow"

Leopoldo María Panero

81

ISO HOOKUP SAYS: wut up lil man!!! wut u doin????

YOUR LORD LATOUR SAYS: Hello.

ISO HOOKUP SAYS: aint seen u 4 days

YOUR LORD LATOUR SAYS: I've been busy.

ISO HOOKUP SAYS: 2 bzy 4 me

YOUR LORD LATOUR SAYS: Excuse me, does "2" mean "too"?

ISO HOOKUP SAYS: oc

A pause

ISO HOOKUP SAYS: zzzzz

YOUR LORD LATOUR SAYS: And the next thing you wrote, I guess, is "of course," while the z's mean that you grew impatient waiting for me to write this answer. Is that right?

ISO HOOKUP SAYS: zzzzz

YOUR LORD LATOUR SAYS: Answer me.

ISO HOOKUP SAYS: dont be so upty

YOUR LORD LATOUR SAYS: Uppity?

ISO HOOKUP SAYS: q pedo sr. 30+!!! :P

Another pause

ISO HOOKUP SAYS: zzzzzzzzzzzz

ISO HOOKUP SAYS: zzzzzzzzzzzzzzzzzzzzzzzzzzzzzzzzz

ISO HOOKUP SAYS: zzzzzzzzzzzzzzzzzzzzzzzzzzzzzzzzzzzzzzzzzzzzz

YOUR LORD LATOUR SAYS: If you are trying to "embarrass me" with the suggestion that I'm over thirty years old, because I refuse to use the abbreviations that you use, it'll be very difficult. Not only because I'm already past thirty, and there is nothing I can or would do in that regard, but also for the following reasons and be thankful that I'll put them in separate notes:

ISO HOOKUP SAYS: zzzzzzzzzzz

YOUR LORD LATOUR SAYS: First, the power that I have and that I wield doesn't depend on my age.

ISO HOOKUP SAYS: dont b an

ISO HOOKUP SAYS: ahole

YOUR LORD LATOUR SAYS: Second, you know perfectly well that my interest in these matters is real and that I really am looking for an obedient person for a relationship. Otherwise, you wouldn't still be talking to me.

ISO HOOKUP SAYS: wow

YOUR LORD LATOUR SAYS: Third, I already know who you are.

Another pause

ISO HOOKUP SAYS: wow so

YOUR LORD LATOUR SAYS: I know you're not a woman.

ISO HOOKUP SAYS: scared

YOUR LORD LATOUR SAYS: And because of everything else I suspect that you're not younger than thirty.

YOUR LORD LATOUR SAYS: You don't sound as real as you think. You try too hard.

Another pause

YOUR LORD LATOUR SAYS: I've talked to you several times. I know you. You think women are all submissive and stupid, but that's how you hide the fact that it's you who wants to be submissive and stupid.

Another pause

Your Lord Latour says: You're still there.

Iso hookup says: y

Your Lord Latour says: Write correctly.

Iso hookup says: yes

Your Lord Latour says: Capitalize yes. And use punctuation. And call me "Sir."

Iso hookup says: Yes, Sir.

Your Lord Latour says: I know you. I've talked to you. Tell me. We've had beautiful fantasies together, haven't we?

Iso hookup says: Yes, Sir.

Iso hookup says: They've been beautiful

Your Lord Latour says: Wait until I'm finished writing and then answer. If I want to leave you there waiting, you'll wait for as long as necessary.

Iso hookup says: Yes, Sir.

Your Lord Latour says: Would you like to stop fooling around, masturbating while looking at your screen? You can stop fantasizing and do what you want to do.

Iso hookup says: Yes, Sir.

Your Lord Latour says: I'm serious.

Another pause

Iso hookup says: I said yes.

Your Lord Latour says: You'll have to do what I tell you, starting with using the ID that I'm going to give you. You'll do what I say. We'll see each other when and where I say.

A very long pause.

Your Lord Latour says: Answer me now, or you won't talk to me again.

Iso hookup says: Yes, Sir.

Your Lord Latour says: Tell me the name of someone you hate and tell me why.

Iso hookup says: Edmundo. My boss. He's a pendejo.

Your Lord Latour says: The name you use to talk to me will be Mundo. Because I want you to. Because you have to know your worth and your place

Latour waited.

Mundo says: I changed it.

Mundo waited, shaking. His teeth were chattering, and he had an enormous erection. His body had never felt like that.

82

"Yes, ow, wait"

Latour ignored him and pushed again.

"It hurts. Ow! Seriously! Hey, wait ...!"

Latour didn't wait. Nor did he stop or decrease the force with which he pushed, once, again, and again.

Mundo complained again, faintly, and then he stayed quiet. He was discovering something in the pain that grew and then settled in a new part of his body. And Latour's insistence and carelessness were different too, and the stench of the room, and the remoteness of the hotel...

83

When they were traveling in one of the cars, Mundo, curled up on the floor, was almost always able to see the streetlights through the window that passed one after another at regular intervals. But he couldn't see any now. That was unusual.

"Where are we going?" Mundo asked.

He waited for the slap or blow with the cane, because he had been ordered to keep quiet. But neither of the two punishments came.

"Aren't you cold?" Latour asked, who was next to him but seated, looking outside.

The question made Mundo feel uneasy, which was also infrequent.

"Come, sit," Latour said, and took Mundo by an arm to encourage him to sit up. After a moment, for the first time during the years he'd been with Latour, Mundo felt the leather of the seat beneath his skin. He touched one of the armrests with his hand. Now, suddenly, he was cold. Latour had looked out again.

Mundo saw that they were traveling along a highway and that the city was now behind him, in the distance.

84

Mundo could see that Andrea wasn't stupid: she understood that something was wrong, and she showed her concern, from the first weeks.

Mundo—he already thought of himself by giving himself that name, as if it were a loving word, assigned in a tender and secret game—knew that they fought less because he was no longer interested in fighting and preferred to avoid it. He even agreed to spend time with the girl—who was unbearable—, who was responsible for changing the baby's diapers and had stopped arguing about its name, the details of the baptism, the in-laws' suggestions.

Once, he even told her:

"Look, I've thought about it now, you're the mother: the children are more the mother's than the father's. They're more the mother's family's. So, then. José Luis is a nice name. Your papá will be happy."

And he smiled when he saw Andrea's bewildered face, who would have preferred (she thought) signals that were easier to decipher. But he almost never stayed until late at the office any longer, he no longer said no to Andrea when she suggested they go out, he no longer avoided telling her the trivial goings-on with his boss or coworkers.

The time he was able to devote to Latour in the office wasn't enough, and sometimes he was able to lock himself in the little study they had fashioned in their apartment and turn on his own computer. Doubtlessly Andrea believed he was staying up all night visiting porn sites, and in reality, the routine didn't vary: he'd ejaculate into pieces of toilet paper that he threw in the toilet and would scrub the browser history so that there was no trace of the sites he frequented.

But now the addresses were more bizarre than before: abandoned forums that no one had removed from the web, that remained buried and deserted except by people like Latour and him. Others who left messages seemed to be members of criminal gangs or traffickers of various types; neither of the two paid attention to them as they shared their fantasy, or told each other, slave and master, how impatient they were to be together. Then, Mundo would clean up, turn off the device, go to the children's room and give them kisses and hugs before going to Andrea's bed.

85

One morning, Mundo looked at himself in a mirror in the basement and discovered that he had lost weight. The fact surprised him; it had only been a few days since the infections in his stomach and legs had healed: it was still possible to see the holes of the shoddily done piercings.

He had stayed in bed—in a bed—for several days, while a discreet doctor and a nurse treated him. Latour had stayed away. And now everything was like in the beginning: the employees of the house ignored him; Latour treated him like always, and they spent several hours together; he had gone back to sleeping on the mat.

But Mundo said: "It takes a lot of courage," and his voice sounded like always. This surprised him too, because he's heard that something happened to people who went a long time without talking. He lay on the floor, like so many other times, to wait for Latour, but he could barely control himself: he raised one hand, the other, a leg, or he arched himself so that his back didn't touch the floor, which seemed frozen to him.

86

"Everything's fine," Latour said, calm, and the car continued down the road.

87

That night he stayed a little longer. It wasn't necessary, but he wanted to be sure that nobody saw him: he was shaking just as he had the first time in front of the screen. He thought he should be happy, excited, at least relieved: no more responsibilities at home, the children's screaming, the arguments.

After a few minutes he got up and walked to bathroom.

As he left, he said:

"It takes courage," and he said it again several times, out loud, to the walls of the corridor, the common area, his cubicle.

When he finally left the office, as they'd agreed, he didn't pick up his car from the parking lot. Instead, he went down to the street and took the bus that Latour had indicated. He was able to find a seat where he sat until the end of the route. An ugly brown-skinned woman who was sleeping with her legs apart in a nearby seat caught his attention; on top of her—in reality, she wasn't supporting her—a very small blonde girl was asleep. Suddenly, the bus came to a stop, and the girl fell to the floor, from where the woman picked her up with a single swift movement, almost without opening her eyes. So Mundo observed that the girl—she had begun to scream because of the pain or out of fright—was as dark as the woman but had dyed hair: she already had almost an inch of black roots.

Mundo got off the bus and became entangled with people who were moving around him. Until now he realized that he had been fighting back something for hours, holding back an impulse that felt like the final aftertaste of vomit in the throat. All he wanted was to go back to the building, pick up his car, go back home and lie in bed with Andrea. He would then change email accounts, change his phone number, deny forever—and in the most reasonable way—that he could ever have had a relationship with the man who was now waiting for him, at the agreed-upon corner, in an old small car, accompanied only by a bodyguard.

He was a mere employee. No one. What would a man like the one who was already opening the door of the car want with him?

Then he thought he was afraid to be free. That he had to be free. That he'd never done anything for himself. That for once he should break his ties and affirm his own worth and his own independence. Andrea was always, always complaining about the same thing. His coworkers complained about the same thing. His son and daughter, when the time came, complained about the same thing.

He wanted to say something, to shout; instead he just got into the car. During the drive, he felt a knot in his throat and cried in silence.

As soon as they were in the house, and the bodyguard had left, Mundo undressed. Then he put on the collar that Latour held out to him and bent down to touch his forehead to the cement floor, just at tips of his master's shoes.

"The boy's already four years old. I don't know what to tell him, so, it's better I don't say anything... Are you there ...? So I tell my mother that in the end we get used to the way things are, and well, yes, yes, it's true. But the other day when you called, he, the boy, Luisito, heard me and asked who it was. And, so, what am I supposed to tell him?"

Mundo was crouched on the floor, away from the table where the phone was. Latour was the one who had dialed, who had brought the receiver to him to say hello and who had pulled him away with a gesture, but both of them must have been, without a doubt, just as surprised: it had been a long time since Andrea was in the mood to talk.

And Mundo could no longer imagine what she was thinking or how things were going for her.

"I can't even tell him to get angry or to go look for you one day so that you can explain to him why..." —a drowned-out, indecipherable sound. "Last month I went again, did I tell you? To the police station. To ask. And again the same thing. You probably left with another woman. Why make a scandal. And when I insisted, when I tried to show them the recordings, the same guy came out, the same one as before, exactly the same one, to say the exactly the same thing... Do you pay him? Does the person you're with pay him? Are you really the one who says I should not get myself into more trouble, that people are helping you"—again the sound—"important people?"

"That's enough," Latour said, and he hung up.

They never called her again, and Mundo never found out if Latour stopped paying everyone responsible for watching Andrea, hindering her investigations, facilitating contact when Latour decided.

The cross was X-shaped, with shackles to immobilize his wrists and ankles. But it was much more uncomfortable than it looked. They only used it a couple of times and then it just stayed there, in the room, along with other discarded toys.

"Hey, Jaime, hey."

Mundo didn't smile; Latour never allowed his guests to use his first name when they were at his home.

"How's it going, Don Genaro? By the way, thanks for inviting me."

"Oh, yes, yes, this is your house, you know. Anytime. So…"

They talked for a few minutes about politics, the weather, Latour's father and his business, Don Genaro's trial, which certainly wouldn't lead to anything but had to take its course. Mundo distracted himself by listening to music or looking at the altarpieces and statues; every once in a while he dared to look at some of the couples who were dancing and the only other slave at the party: a tiny, thin girl, naked like him, with a similar leash, at the feet of a severe-looking woman who occasionally pinched her nose or cheek.

Finally, the man—the old man: he seemed even more repulsive to Mundo in person than in photographs—slipped an arm over Latour's shoulder and approached him to say:

"And you never want to get yourself…, no offense, eh? uh… Jaime, son, how do you say to your friend…?"

"Don't talk to him, he'll get bored," Latour said. Mundo, lying on the rug next to the armchair, gently rubbed (with his face, like a cat) one of his legs.

"No offense to him," the old man said to Latour, "but tell me, honestly, do you really like it that much? What do you see in it? Excuse me," the man told Mundo.

"What can I say, Don Genaro? We all," Latour said, "like different things."

"Well, yes, the flesh is weak," the other man said, and took a sip of his whiskey. "I know I'm not the one to criticize anyone, but... Wouldn't you like... more...a...?"

He gestured with his hands. Mundo didn't know how to decipher it, but he knew numerous details about the man, the story about his trials and testimonies: he had been living with Latour for barely three months, and he still remembered what he'd read in the newspapers.

"Someone younger?" Latour said.

Mundo didn't change positions.

"Well, yes. You're still young, but your... well, he's not my age but he's not a youngster."

"I've never liked children."

Mundo remained still, glued to Latour's leg.

"Well, I don't understand why," said the old man, laughing, and Latour laughed too. "I guess it's a matter of trust, right?"

"He doesn't have many options," Latour said, and began to slap Mundo's ear. "Isn't that right, you?"

Mundo didn't know how to answer.

"Listen, by the way, Don Genaro," Latour said, still slapping Mundo's ear, "I wanted to ask, while we're on the subject. He speaks, even if it doesn't seem like it, and although he appears to be an idiot, the truth is, sometimes we talk about... well, things."

"Yes?"

"We talk a lot. He's not very educated but he understands. We talk about beauty. Do you ever talk with...?"

He didn't finish. Mundo could see the old man's face and understood his expression to be one of displeasure.

"No, no," he heard him say. "Of course not. I'm an older man, with life experience... Sometimes I ask them to pray... I like their voices."

Later that night, the woman's slave took advantage of a minute to crawl on the ground and get close to him. Mundo thought she would speak to him but she confined herself to sniffing him and, after a moment, licking his nose.

91

The rubber uniform was a double disappointment: there was an error in the first shipment, and a woman's suit arrived, with room for breasts, too narrow at the waist, and then the mistake was repeated in three subsequent shipments, over a period of weeks. Latour was furious; Mundo chose to seek refuge in the tiny room where he was allowed to sleep on colder nights; he spent hours on the cot, under the sheet, looking at the ceiling or fantasizing. He would have liked a TV set, or at least something to listen to music, but didn't dare go out and ask for it: once in a while, in the distance, he heard screams.

And when the suit finally arrived, and Mundo put it on—it was a beautiful, black garment with no visible openings, and it stuck to the skin and clung to it exactly like Mundo had always imagined—the two began to play but Mundo suffocated after a few minutes. The rubber had to be cut so he could get out. That night, Latour burned the four suits at the bottom of the roofed pool, which he ordered to be drained (Mundo understood) for the occasion: he hadn't anticipated that when the material burned it would throw off so much smoke, rendering the place unusable for almost a month.

92

The girl danced like the others, holding onto one of the tubes, but Latour pointed at her and said:

"I call her Shit. I chose it. That's what I call her, and she loves it."

She was tall and ungainly, with very short arms for the size of her torso and a strange face: her nose was too small and her eyes were too far apart.

Mundo didn't understand, at that moment, what Latour was trying to tell him. He was intrigued: they almost never went to specialty places, made exclusively for people with their tastes, and even less often to markets. And this was a luxury store. All the customers were like Latour, beautiful and slender and confident, and everyone else looked healthy, very willing, with genuine smiles.

"Tell me. What do you think?"

Mundo, a bit surprised, cleared his throat.

93

"Say something."

"Yes. Yes. Yes, Sir."

Mundo buried his face into the pillow. He could detect the odor of his own sweat but also, underneath, the smell of the fabric. It reminded him of his childhood. Without being tied to any particular memory, the smell made him think of long nights, in his room, the silent discharges onto the carpet, which were never cleaned.

"More, please, Sir, more," he pleaded.

94

When leaving a party, Latour pointed out an older man to Mundo, with white hair and thick glasses, who was accompanied by a boy dressed in black tie. He didn't bother to hide: he pointed to them with his finger and said out loud:

"Look. That one there is also a slave. The boy with the bowtie."

The two stared at Latour and Mundo.

"The only thing is the slave doesn't get naked until he gets home. He's a hypocrite. And his owner too."

The two rushed out of the house and got into the car that was waiting for them. Latour lingered to chat with the party's hostess, who wanted to sell something to Latour. Mundo never found out what it was:

"The Sultan loved them when he came. I'm sure you'll love them too," she said.

"Send ten to my house," Latour replied, but if the ten arrived Mundo didn't find out. Of course, it could have been something related to Latour's affairs: the occasions when he would go out in suit and tie, and would leave him locked in the basement, tied up somewhere, with some device inserted or his face painted or some feather and stone setup.

95

The car stopped at the gutter.

"Get out," Latour said.

Mundo looked at Latour and then the driver, who continued to look ahead. He got out of the car. It was starting to rain. The driver got out with an umbrella with which he shielded

Latour.

"Get up."

Mundo stood up. The rain was freezing. He wanted to move toward Latour but, before he could do it, Latour said:

"Take off your collar."

"What?"

Mundo looked to one side and then the other. Then he was forced to say:

"What is my master saying?"

"Take it off," Latour insisted, and as Mundo obeyed, he added: "This is where we say goodbye. You're staying here. I don't want

114

to see you again, so don't come back, understood?" Now. Go. Away.

Mundo didn't move. He couldn't. The rain continued to fall, and the only thing he could see, beyond Latour and the driver, were the headlights, which reflected and broke apart in the puddles.

96

"Señora, it's me, Fernando."

The woman hung up. Mundo dialed again. The third time, he heard, away from the receiver, the voice of Andrea, who was shouting something.

"Señora, please, señora, listen to me," Mundo said. "I know they've spoken to you before, but they've... kidnapped me, they're making me, they're pointing a gun at me. Please, please help me."

But he couldn't continue because he started to laugh. Latour hung up the phone.

"Was it that funny?" he asked. "Can't you be serious? Does it get the best of you? Does laughter get the best of you?" And he took off his belt, which was leather and had a heavy buckle.

Mundo was scared, but he couldn't do that part of the routine well: he said thank you after each blow and withdrew to be attended to by one of the servants.

97

"There is," Latour concluded, "beauty simply in bending others to your will," and he put down the sheet of paper.

Mundo had already figured out that, on some occasions, other people were responsible for writing for him.

"If my master will allow me, it would sound, well, more confident without the 'like'."

"Didn't you see it was a poem? If I take out words the verse loses its meter."

"May my master forgive me," Mundo asked, and touched the floor with his forehead.

"Then, yes, it's good?"

"As my master says."

"No, tell me seriously!"

Mundo thought about what he could say and remembered something that he had read in a magazine or maybe heard in high school, long ago.

"Perhaps you can put another word, my master, that is, instead of 'like,' so the meter remains the same."

Latour stared at the paper.

"No," he said. "No. You do it if you want," and he threw the paper on the floor.

98

"I'm telling you to talk. What do you think?"

"I like it," Mundo shouted, to be heard over the music." I like that there's a place like this. I like that there are people who come and do this and feel good, that aren't hypocrites. And I like that it's well-to-do people, not dirty. Everyone thinks all this is dirty, but you can see here..."

"Yes, yes, okay, okay, okay. Sit down," Latour ordered, and Mundo sat on the floor. "Let's see, you're dead," and Mundo played dead, with his arms folded and legs raised. "Spin around."

As he spun around, Mundo brushed the arm of a man with his legs. The beer bottle he was holding spilled on his chest. The man stood up, turned to look at Mundo, saw that he was naked and wear a dog collar, and looked up at Latour.

"Hey," he began to say, irritated, but as soon as he saw who he was talking to, fell silent and went back to his table.

"I asked you what you thought about Shit," Latour said. She's younger, prettier..."

"What does my master say?" Mundo asked. Latour had spoken quietly.

99

"What has displeased my master?" Mundo shouted.

Latour moved his leg but Mundo didn't let go.

"It's not that anything..." he began.

"Doesn't my master want to...?"

"Don't talk like that."

"My master likes it."

"Enough. It even seems like you are..."

"I am what my master wants me to be. I do what he tells me, I say what he tells me, I think what he tells me. My body is for what he tells me. My..."

Latour struggled but managed to push Mundo away with a kick. He fell back and didn't get up. Instead, he stared at him from the ground. He was surprised by everything: he hadn't seen it coming.

"Well," Latour said, "it could have been worse. You could have started to talk normally. I would have seen that you don't take any of this seriously..."

Mundo felt relieved. He sniffled loudly, like a child, and knelt again. He kissed Latour's shoes, he licked them, he barely felt the kick in the mouth that caused him to fall backward.

"My master knows," he said, looking at the asphalt, "that this is serious for me. That I left everything for my master. That I've been good and obedient. That I'm stupid and that I'm..."

"I'll give you money. Okay? For your time."

Mundo didn't look up.

After a moment, he heard the door of the car close. He wanted to look: the car was already making a U-turn to return to where it had come from.

He looked for his collar, which he'd dropped, but couldn't find it.

100

At dawn, trembling, frozen by the rain that was still falling, he managed to stop a car. At first, he didn't know what to tell them: then he explained that someone had mugged him and left him there. They threw a jacket on him and took him to a town he'd never seen. They went down into a fonda on the outskirts of town, and they handed him a towel. They also placed a telephone in front of him: he understood that they expected him to call someone to come pick him up.

He dialed the number he knew, the only one: all the others La-tour had dialed, as they moved around. A voice he didn't recognize answered. He hung up without answering.

The car's drivers had already left. The owner of the fonda looked at his crotch, which was uncovered. He tried to remember some-one else's number, but before he could think of anyone who could help him, he realized his situation wasn't so desperate. Even if he didn't remember anyone's information, if he didn't get any money to get out of there in a bus or a taxi, he could ask the woman to lend him, anything, used clothes and some old shoes, and walk. It might take the whole day, and the trip would definitely exhaust him, but he would go back to the city, and there he would find someone, someone who had known him before: he would even go to the of-fice, ask for help, make something up.

But, suddenly, he understood that he didn't want to do that. He didn't want to see anyone. He didn't want to find Andrea, or An-drea's family, or Andrea's children. He didn't want to go back to work. He didn't want to return to his previous life as if nothing had happened. He didn't like women. He didn't like to play the role of a father, be the strong man. He didn't like taking care of others.

Suddenly he was distracted by the fonda's owner, who threw a pair of old pants in his face.

"Cover yourself up!"

Mundo put on the pants.

He was going to, he thought, return to Latour. At least to see him one more time, to make him see everything he had lost.

"Thank you," he said to the woman, and then, because he felt like it, he continued: "I'm going back, I'm going to find him, wherever he is, and I'll tell him the truth. I'll tell him he's never going to find anyone like me. That he'll soon see. That it's his loss."

He didn't speak for a moment.

Then he said: "It's his loss. That's it. It's his loss."

He was free. He was completely free. And he had the courage to be free. Who was going to stop him?

101

Back at home, Latour goes outside to look at the garden and feigns a dramatic moment. Standing under the umbrella, he lifts his chin and tries to look at the sky. He recoils at the first drop that falls onto his face and then sighs. He imagines his own face, in profile, against a sky that isn't the city's, blackened by still thick, swollen clouds, but from a movie: blue and pregnant with stars.

He doesn't know if Mundo might be capable of returning, of even finding the site, but he's already given the order that he not be permitted to enter: other slaves have tried, but the cries, the reproaches, the fits of crying and anger no longer interest him. Not even the violent and ugly beating his security detail is capable of giving—he knows this—would excite him: since the death of Sylph, the fourth or fifth of his "spiteful lovers," no violence has seemed the same to him. Every first time implies a thousand disappointments later; he no longer fools himself about his capacity for boredom, nor about the fact that real happiness is forever fleeting.

After a moment, he remembers that the one who died wasn't Sylph but Omar. Sylph came later. How long has he spent on these quests? The only detail he has repeated since the first times (from Pollito, the Twins, Brenda) is dumping them completely naked, without anything, and even that, now, means nothing to him. What's more, he didn't understand the expression on Mundo's face when the car started without him, and that bothers him: was there something, some character trait about that poor idiot that Latour never knew?

"No," he says out loud. "No. No, of course not."

He feels restless. But, precisely because of this, he doesn't resist the notion of some sentimental music, light and pretentious, like the kind that accompanies life lessons and sentimental revelations in the movies or on television.

Surrounded by music, without saying anything more, and before the names of the actors begin to appear on the screen, he remembers that his new slave is already waiting for him. Latour enters the house and closes the door. 🕀

Acknowledgments

THIS BOOK is indebted to Carlos Bortoni, who first challenged me to tackle a "realist" writing project all the way back in 2008 (Nabokov used to say that the word "reality" should always go in quotation marks); to Bernardo Fernández Bef, a constant friend; to Carlos Velázquez, perhaps the earliest reviewer and champion the novel had during its Mexican run; to Omar, Michele, and George, its new godparents.

And to Raquel, as always, for everything. ⊞

A. C.
Mexico City

Epigraphs

a) From the novel *Dangerous Liaisons*. Translated by Helen Constantine and published by Penguin Classics.

c) From the novel *Jakob von Gunten*. Translated by Christopher Middleton and published by New York Review Books.

b) From the poem "Home Economics," in *A Rosario Castellanos Reader*. Translated by Maureen Ahern for the University of Texas Press.

d) From the poem "Mutis." Translated by Arthur Dixon. ⯒

About the Author

ALBERTO CHIMAL (Toluca, 1970) is a Mexican fiction author, as well as a noted teacher of creative-writing. One of his main areas of interest is the *fantastic imagination* —a Latin American mode quite different from the English-language *fantasy* genre— which he has employed in his award-winning novels and short stories.

These awards include the Premio Bellas Artes de Cuento San Luis Potosí (Mexico's National Short Story Prize, 2002); the Premio de Literatura Estado de México (the State of Mexico Literary Prize, 2012); the Premio Colima de Narrativa (Colima Narrative Prize, 2013) and the Premio Fundación Cuatrogatos Prize (Cuatrogatos Foundation Prize, 2016), which recognizes the best children's and YA literature written in Spanish. Moreover, children's picture book *La madre y la muerte / La partida* (which features a story by Chimal and another by Argentinian writer Alberto Laiseca) was selected for inclusion in the International Youth Library's White Ravens Catalogue of the best children's/YA fiction of 2016. Additionally, his Twitter novel *City X* received the Best Short Story Prize by Speculative Fiction in Translation in 2018; and his second novel, *La torre y el jardín*, was shortlisted in 2013 for the Rómulo Gallegos International Novel Prize, one of the Spanish language's most prestigious awards.

Chimal's work explores a range of themes, forms, styles, and genres considered unusual for Mexican writers. In addition to fiction, he has published essays, plays, articles, translations, as well as two creative writing manuals. Together with the director Jorge Michel Grau, he co-authored the screenplay 7:19, *la hora del temblor* (2016), the first realistic drama to be made about the catastrophic earthquake that devastated Mexico City in 1985, a mayor event in that country's history.

Since 1993, Chimal has taught literature and creative writing to hundreds of students and aspiring writers, many of whom have gone on to earn national and international recognition. He holds a Master's Degree in Comparative Literature from the Universidad Nacional Autónoma de México. His works have been translated into numerous languages, including English, French, Italian, German, Hungarian, Farsi, Hebrew, Mixe, Zapotec, Mixtec, and Esperanto. He lives in Mexico City with his wife, author Raquel Castro, with whom he hosts a YouTube channel about books, creative writing, and similar topics.

Alberto Chimal is represented by VF Agencia Literaria. Please visit its contact page (vfagencialiteraria.com/contacto) for inquiries. ⌗

www.ingramcontent.com/pod-product-compliance
Lightning Source LLC
Chambersburg PA
CBHW021926170626
46807CB00007B/2998